CONVOY TO CATASTROPHE

Submarine WWII Series
Book Four

Charles Whiting
writing as
Leo Kessler

SAPERE
BOOKS

CONVOY TO CATASTROPHE

Published by Sapere Books.

24 Trafalgar Road, Ilkley, LS29 8HH

saperebooks.com

ISBN: 978-0-85495-137-6

'Twas on a summer's day — the sixth of June;
     I like to be particular in dates,
  Not only of the age, and year, but moon;
They are a sort of post-house, where the Fates
Change horses, making history change its tune.
  Then spur away o'er empires and o'er states,
Leaving at last not much besides chronology…
'Twas on the sixth of June, about the hour of
  Half-past six — perhaps still nearer seven.
        Lord Byron; Don Juan

PREFACE

Of course, there is no monument to what *really* happened off this lonely winter coast over forty years ago now. The official US plinth stands there naturally, just off the sand-swept coastal road, photographed by thousands of visitors in the summer when that part of Devon is swamped by holidaymakers from the capital.

'This memorial was presented by the United States Army ... to the people of the South Hams ... generously left their homes and their lands ... to provide a battle practise area ... for the successful assault on Normandy in June 1944 ... their actions resulted in the saving of many hundreds of lives...'

And so it did. On the morning of 6 June, 1944 when the US Fourth Infantry Division, 'the Ivy League', hit the beach code-named 'Utah' in Normandy, their casualties were exactly twelve dead. But who knew then that a mere six weeks before, *in thirty-eight disastrous minutes 638 young American soldiers died violently in a rehearsal for that great assault!*

But there was even more to it than that. On that April night, with the quarter moon hanging low over the sea, when the E-boats had come skimming in, guns pounding so surprisingly, the whole fate of the invasion of Europe hung in the balance. The next morning, after the tragedy had occurred, the whole area for miles around was sealed off. Divers and frogmen were everywhere. On the beach, littered with the dead young men in olive drab, high-ranking officers from General Eisenhower's staff went from corpse to corpse, checking them out. *Were they any of those key men who knew the great secret?*

In London the planners who had been working on the great assault for years now held their breath. Was all their work in vain? Did the Germans know the plan now? At Montgomery's headquarters near Portsmouth, the grave faced generals seriously decided the whole operation should be cancelled. The risk was too great. There would be — *could be* — no invasion in 1944. They would have to start all over again. It was a moment of history, one that could have changed the whole fate of Western Europe, perhaps the world. *Had that lone U-boat, which had been spotted surfacing after the tragedy, with the cold sea still full of panicked, struggling men, taken one single member of the initiated with it, back to Germany and the Gestapo who could make even the bravest man talk after a while…? HAD IT?*

This, then, is the untold story of what happened that April night over forty years ago — the story of *CONVOY TO CATASTROPHE…*

Leo Kessler, Wittlich, April 1985

BOOK ONE: THE BIGOTS

'In war-time, truth is so precious that she should always be surrounded by a bodyguard of lies.'
Winston Churchill

CHAPTER 1

'*Gentlemen, may I have your attention, please?*' The public address system crackled into harsh metallic life, drowning the hiss and slither of the surf. On the beach bloated seagulls rose in protest, crying plaintively like lost children. '*Will you raise — please — your binoculars now — ten o'clock please. They're coming in — NOW!*' And even the tannoy system could not quite disguise the excitement in the speaker's voice.

Obediently the Top Brass, standing on the little road that ran the length of the English beach, raised their heavy glasses and focused them on the grey billows of the smoke-screen rolling across the dull green surface of the sea. Next to the heavy-set divisional commander, Eisenhower ordered an aide, 'All right, Butch, start timing them as soon as they come out of the smoke-screen!'

The divisional commander started to look nervous.

With startling suddenness a Spitfire, bearing the new white stars of the Invasion attack force hurtled across the sea, going all out at four hundred miles an hour.

'Goddammit to hell!' Eisenhower cursed and ducked instinctively as the British plane zoomed over their heads and raced towards Slapton, machine guns chattering. 'What the Sam Hill do they want to come in that low — '

'Sir,' the aide cried urgently, '*here they come!*'

Eisenhower forgot the Spitfire. Hastily he focused his glasses as the fat grey slugs of the tank-landing craft began edging their blunt noses out of the white smoke. 'Get timing, Butch!' he yelled above the roar of their engines.

Next to him the heavy-set divisional commander tensed and flung a furtive glance at his own watch. He said a quick prayer that this landing wouldn't be as fouled up as the last one his Fourth Infantry Division had carried out here on Slapton Sands two weeks before. Christ, they'd even managed to run one of the LSTs aground. Brother, hadn't that been a real snafu!

'As you know, gentlemen,' the officer running the PA system lectured the Top Brass, staring mesmerized out to sea, where the tank-landing craft were already beginning to lower their ramps. 'Slapton Sands, Devon, England has been selected as our main training centre for the coming Invasion because it closely resembles one of the real Invasion beaches in Occupied France, which, in the interest of security, I can tell you only is code-named "Utah".'

Eisenhower nodded his head in approval, not taking his gaze off the ugly tank-landing ships wallowing in the shallows now. If he was going to surprise Rommel's Krauts on the other side of the Channel, the tightest security possible was essential.

Behind him, Butch took his eyes off his stop-watch and announced, '*Five minutes, General*!'

The big divisional commander cursed to himself. They were already two minutes behind schedule. If this was the real thing, the Krauts would already be blasting all hell out of the Invasion fleet. Out there the LSTs were sitting ducks. The Krauts would slaughter his poor guys of the Fourth Infantry.

'Here come the infantry!' the tannoy announced. 'The theory is that they will come in slightly after the tanks. The armour —'

'Crap on the theory!' Eisenhower exploded angrily, face red with sudden fury. 'Where are the frigging tanks? They haven't even got the ramps down!'

The big divisional commander experienced that old, old sinking feeling. It was going to be yet another snafu…

Now the first infantry started pounding up the gravel, their faces purple with the effort, eyes wild, wide and bulging. To the right, up in the deserted village of Slapton, and from the left at the hotel on the point, machine guns opened up. White tracer zipped lethally just above the heads of the running men.

'Today we are using live ammo,' the man on the tannoy announced almost proudly, 'in order to get the men used to the real thing. The tightest possible security measures are being taken to ensure casualties are kept as low as possible. All our machine gunners are trained marksmen —'

Down on the beach, one of the infantry yelped with pain and sat down abruptly, white hand clasped tightly to his shoulder, bright red blood seeping through his fingers. The divisional commander groaned.

'*Ten minutes, General.*' Butch intoned.

'Where are those frigging tanks?' Eisenhower moaned.

Now the infantry were flinging themselves at the wire full tilt. Here and there men screamed as the cruel barbs dug into their soft flesh. But already other men were using their impaled, spread-eagled bodies as human bridges and dropping over the other side of the barbed wire obstacles. '*At the double, men… Move yer goddam keesters … at the double now!*' their officers shrieked above the roar of tank engines, as the first waterproofed Shermans began crawling down the ramps of the tank-landing craft and started nosing their way into the sea.

The divisional commander mentally crossed his fingers, praying that none of them would stall and sink like they had done last time they had rehearsed the attack on Utah beach.

Now the infantry, attacking the beach defences, were hurling grenades at the pillboxes as they spat a deadly hail of lead, while others slid forward in a series of wild dives, lugging their cumbersome Bangalore torpedoes with them, aiming to thrust them under the triple line of apron wire defending the approaches to the pillboxes.

'*Fifteen minutes, General*,' Butch called.

'Yeah,' Eisenhower snarked bitterly, 'and there isn't one single goddam tank on the frigging beach as yet…' He stopped suddenly, face aghast.

To his immediate front one of the Shermans had suddenly disappeared. Abruptly its engine had stopped and now it was gone, right to the bottom of the sea, the only sign of its passing an obscene bubble of trapped air exploding on the green surface.

'The fortunes of war, sir,' the divisional commander said a little helplessly, fat face worried and despondent at the same time.

'Fortunes of war *my ass*!' Eisenhower snorted angrily. 'It's a goddam snafu, that's what it is, Tubby. *A right royal snafu*!'

Miserably General 'Tubby' Barton, Commander of the Fourth US Infantry Division, agreed with the Supreme Commander. *Situation normal, all fucked up*, otherwise known as 'snafu', that it very definitely was. He waited for the rocket to come…

'Okay,' Eisenhower snapped, lighting yet another of the sixty Lucky Strikes he chain-smoked each day, 'this is the deal. Your combat engineers, Tubby, did a damn fine job of work!' He indicated the men sprawled out in the wet sand around the Mere, chests heaving from the effort, crimson faces glazed with sweat in spite of the cold wind sweeping in from over the sea. Out there they were already beginning to dive for the lost Sherman tank, but everyone present knew the tankers didn't stand a chance. Even as they stood there listening to the Supreme Commander, the four-man crew was slowly choking to death beneath the surface of the English Channel.

'Your infantry was fair, Tubby,' Eisenhower continued. 'But they are still not fast enough. They were at least five minutes late hitting the beaches, and I don't have to tell you that in those five minutes a lot of fine young men are gonna get slaughtered on the day.'

Barton nodded his head miserably. He knew that, too.

'The real snafu, of course, was your support tanks. Instead of coming in *in front* of the infantry, they were *way back* of them — and Tubby, that is a goddam recipe for disaster!' The Supreme Commander took an angry puff of his cigarette, threw it away, and immediately lit another with a GI Zippo lighter.

All of them waited patiently while he did so, ignoring the sheeplike *baa*ing of the infantry who now wanted to be taken back to their camps for the hot chow and coffee that was waiting for them there. Far, far out to sea there came the muted drone of an engine, whether that of a plane or some patrolling motor torpedo, securing the training area, no one knew or cared at that moment. All attention was focused on the broad-faced Supreme Commander with his wide mouth, known to movie audiences all over the Free World as being set in a big grin; but today fixed in a hard, angry, unyielding grimace.

Eisenhower fussed with his Zippo lighter and then finally got the cigarette lit. He took a deep satisfying drag and said softly so that the lower ranking officers at the edge of the group could not hear, 'There is just one other thing, Tubby — *security*!'

'Security, sir?' the divisional commander asked, a little puzzled. 'I don't quite follow you, sir.'

Eisenhower took the other man by the arm and steered him away from the rest. 'You got Bigots in the assault force, Tubby?' he hissed.

The drone was becoming louder. Out at sea, someone gave a sharp order over the ship's PA system. Neither the Supreme Commander nor 'Tubby' Barton seemed to hear.

'*Bigots*, sir!' Barton echoed. 'Why yes, sir, I think we have. Both the battalion commanders of the combat engineers and my First Battalion know where —' he stopped urgently, as if he'd just burnt his tongue '— are Bigots, sir,' he corrected himself hastily.

Eisenhower nodded and took another deep drag of his Lucky Strike, eyes narrowed to slits, as he absorbed the information. Out at sea, sailors were racing to their action stations everywhere in the Invasion fleet. Whistles started to shrill. Aldis lamps began to clack urgent signals from one boat to another. On the big grey cruiser anchored out in the sound, the guns began to move slowly skywards to meet the challenge. Still the two generals did not notice.

'Well, Tubby, what say one of those Bigots had gotten washed out to sea during the exercise? And what say a Kraut E-boat had been waiting out there for just such an eventuality? And what say the Krauts got our Bigot back to France and handed him over to the Gestapo?' He stared directly at the heavy-set divisional commander. 'What then, Tubby?' His eyes bored fiercely into the other man's fat face. '*Eh?*'

Barton stared at the Supreme Commander aghast. 'Why, sir, that would mean,' he stuttered, 'that —'

'We'd have to cancel the whole goddam Invasion!' Eisenhower interrupted him bitterly. 'The Krauts would know everything and we would have to start all over again. And God only knows what they would be able to pull out of the hat by the time we got that far again. We already know about their damn rockets, aimed at London,' he added sombrely, as the first dark, ominous shapes appeared on the horizon and the guns of the fleets moved round to meet the challenge. 'Christ, they could have all sorts of nasty tricks up their sleeves. Poison gas, anthrax — *anything*!' Eisenhower pulled himself together hastily. He knew he simply could not allow the possibility of the Invasion *not* taking place in this summer of 1944. It would mean the end of his meteoric career. Washington would not forgive him. 'No, Tubby,' he said firmly, 'we can't take the slightest chance. This is what I want you to do.'

'Sir,' Barton snapped. Now he could hear the snarl of racing plane engines out to sea quite plainly. It was probably yet another of the Kraut 'tip-and-run' raids which they had been putting in all along the English south coast these last few weeks. There seemed little purpose to the minor raids save to frighten elderly English gentlefolk living out their old age in places like Bognor Regis and Torquay. What damage could a couple of Focke-Wulfs in a hurry really do?

'Those two Bigots — and all the Bigots in your Division, for that matter — I want them under constant guard when they are engaged in missions such as this.'

'What kind of guard, sir?'

'*Armed guard, dammit*!' Eisenhower snapped as over at the fleet the flak opened up and the dark shapes of the two German dive-bombers were suddenly hurtling through a black and grey network of exploding shells. 'And listen, Tubby,' he added urgently.

'Sir.'

'If there is the slightest danger, even the mere suspicion of one, that your Bigots are going to end up in Jerry hands, you are', he raised his voice against the roar of the planes, as they came skidding over the surface of the water, their racing radial engines whipping up the sea below into an angry white, '*to shoot them in cold blood*! And that's an order. Now let's get the hell out of here…'

With an ear-splitting thundering, the 190s zoomed over the prostrate figures hugging the wet sand, their machine guns chattering frantically, while high, high above the beach, that beautiful plane circled round and round gracefully, snapping photo after photo…

CHAPTER 2

Kapitänleutnant Christian Jungblut moaned softly and slowly, very slowly, opened his oil-scummed eyes. Beneath him the raft rocked gently in the swell. Cautiously through the slits he gazed at the horizon. Just as it had been for the last terrible two days it was empty save for the unbearable glare of the tropical sun.

Almost as if it weighed a hundredweight, he raised his arm, now burned black by the sun in the parts not covered by the caked oil scum, and shaded his eyes.

The other raft, which the night before had been half submerged under the weight of the other survivors of the ill-fated U-82, had vanished. In its place there was big black floating mass like jelly about ten or twelve centimetres thick, in the middle of which floated a 'something'; a blackened log which had once been a human being.

Suddenly it came flooding back — *everything*. The way the Ami Catalinas had caught them on the surface as they had been refuelling from the Jap tanker. The sudden hail of bombs. The great blowtorch of flame which had swept the length of the tanker, carrying over to the U-82, transforming his poor sailors into hunched, charred pygmies in an instant. The panic-stricken flight over the side. Men chucking tables, floats, pieces of wood — anything — in their frenzied haste to escape that killing flame…

For twenty-four hours the iron discipline of the German U-boat Service had kept them sane. But then the parched survivors had started drinking sea water, even their own urine. He had seen two men urinating into each other's mouths in a desperate attempt to obtain liquid! Thereafter they had started going mad. Some simply dived from their makeshift floats, crying happily, 'Just swimming over to the islands, comrades… Get myself a nice cold mug of suds!' Franz, the one-time Bavarian farmhand, had yelled in his thick country accent, 'Must milk old Strawberry! It's way past her milking-time,' and he had dived over the side urgently and had begun swimming in fine style until his strength had given out and he had disappeared beneath the waves of the Indian Ocean without a sound. Others had whispered through parched, cracked lips, 'Good luck, comrades… All the best,' and had slipped over the sides to their death, before anyone could stop them…

By nightfall the day before, there had been only two rafts left, the one he shared with *Obermaat* Frenssen, and the other one packed with the remaining survivors. Now it was gone and he was alone. *Or was he?*

He started up, only to feel a big hand like a small steam-shovel pressed against his chest, full of gentle pressure. 'It's all right, sir … all right,' Frenssen said soothingly in that familiar waterfront accent of his. 'I'm still here — *just*!' He gave a throaty chuckle, which ended in a sudden burst of coughing, and Christian could hear the Hamburger vomiting over the side of the frail little craft. Obviously he too had swallowed some of that damned diesel oil.

Slowly, as if his head were worked by rusty springs, Christian turned towards where the big petty officer in his oil-splattered, charred overalls retched miserably, washing his mouth out with a little seawater, spitting it out almost immediately, after each bout of vomiting. 'Bad?' he croaked.

Frenssen turned and wiped the tears from his red-rimmed eyes. 'Only when I laugh, sir,' he answered. Again he took in his skipper's appearance; the face haggard and hollowed out to a grey death's head, the eyes scummed and almost closed with oil-waste. Abruptly he forgot his own misery. Taking a nail he had worked loose from the boards of the raft during the night, he began to dig and tear at the kapok of his life-belt. For a moment or two Christian stared at him in sudden horror. Had the sea water affected the big petty officer too? Surely old Frenssen, who had been with him ever since he had first joined the old U-69 as a cadet, still wet behind the spoons, was not going mad?

Frenssen saw the look of horror on his skipper's face and said hastily, 'No sir, I'm not ready for the funny farm yet. The little fellers in the white coats are not gonna get me in their rubber van — not this week, at least.' He chuckled harshly and opening his flies urinated on the handful of kapok he managed to free from the belt. 'Hold tight, sir, I'm going to try to get that shit out of yer eyes. Sorry about the piss, sir,' he added hastily. 'Why, it ain't even good German beer-piss. Just a mixture of stale sea water and that Jap muck, *saki*, we took on board at Saigon. Now here goes.' Tenderly, like a mother tending a beloved baby, he began to clear the caked oil and dirt from the officer's clogged eyes, while on the horizon the sun started to ascend in all its yellow-glowing fury. It was going to be another scorchingly hot day...

'*Kapitänleutnant* Jungblut,' the Big Lion had barked just before they had set sail four weeks before, 'your mission is of the utmost importance. You might ask, what pickings are there for the U-boat arm in the Indian Ocean when we are having the greatest difficulty in maintaining our position in the Atlantic against the damned Tommies with their newfangled radar? The short answer is none. Besides, the Japanese are responsible for that area of operations against the enemy. No, my dear

Jungblut,' he had rasped, his thin-lipped, cruel mouth working as if on tight steel springs, 'that is not the purpose of your mission. You are one of my most experienced surviving commanders. It will be your duty to show the flag out there.'

Jungblut had allowed himself a mild protest. 'But why, sir? To what purpose? I feel it is my duty —'

'Your duty is to do what I command you to do, *Kapitänleutnant* Jungblut!' the Big Lion had cut him off savagely. 'Now listen, you know as well as I do how we are fighting with our backs against the wall. The Reds are beating us in the East and the Anglo-Americans will attack across the Channel any day now. It is essential that we hang on until the new revenge weapons the Führer has promised us make their appearance. Then we will pay back those Anglo-American air gangsters tenfold for the damage and suffering they have inflicted on our cities.'

Inwardly, Christian had groaned. How often had he heard this old, old story about the 'wonder weapons' in these last terrible months. But where were the damned things, if they really existed? The Third Reich was on its knees, out for a count of nine, and all the fighting men heard was damned *talk … talk … talk*!

The Big Lion must have realized what was going through Christian's mind from the look on his harshly handsome face, for he had snapped sharply, 'They are not just figments of the imagination of Goebbels, the Poison Dwarf, you know, Jungblut. They really *do* exist!'

'Yessir,' he had answered, his voice neutral, unconvinced.

'But they *do*,' the Big Lion had roared in a sudden temper, pounding on the big desk in front of him. 'We have several new kinds of rockets, which I have seen myself. They will soon give London, perhaps even New York, a taste of the kind of punishment from the air we have been receiving for the last two years.' The Big Lion's voice had lowered so that he was speaking almost in a whisper, as if he feared that someone might be listening in the outer office. 'And we of the U-Boat Force have the new Century class U-boat, Jungblut.'

Suddenly he had looked at the younger officer, a kind of hectic gloating suffusing his hard skinny face like that which might spread across the homely features of some provincial virgin announcing to her surprised girlfriends that she was about to lose that frustrating little piece of membrane.

'*Century class, sir*?' he had stuttered. 'Why I've never heard of —'

The Big Lion had held up his hand for silence. 'Of course you haven't, and you will hear no more of our newest weapon until you return from your patrol with the Japanese. But I will speed you on your way with this great news, Jungblut. Complete your patrol successfully and you will be the first commander of the new Century class boats.' He had leaned forward and had hissed, eyes glittering fanatically, 'And remember this, Jungblut, the Century class are war-winners! There is nothing like them in any navy in the whole wide world.' And with that the Big Lion, otherwise known as Admiral Karl Dönitz, head of the German U-Boat Force, had dismissed the bewildered young skipper with an urgent wave of his hand. Even as he had saluted and made for the door, the Admiral had forgotten him, his head bent yet once again over the papers which littered his big desk that had once belonged to Grand Admiral Tirpitz himself…

In the few days they spent in the former French colonial capital, the Japanese naval officers who had come to inspect the U-82 and had expressed their admiration for the German submarine with a great deal of bowing and sharp intakes of breath were exceedingly polite and helpful; yet underneath it all, Christian had sensed their contempt for their white allies. Their underlying brutality was all too obvious too.

Everywhere in Saigon were the captive soldiers of the defeated Allied armies — Australians, English, Dutchmen — skeleton-thin, hollow-eyed, ravaged by malaria and dysentery, many with open sores on their yellow, emaciated bodies, dressed just in loincloths or tatters. These walking skeletons laboured all day under the merciless sun on a handful of wet rice and a cup of thin soup, falling like flies by the end of their shifts to be beaten to their feet again by sadistic guards armed with bamboo canes.

More than once Christian had just managed to restrain one of his angry crewmen from lashing out at some grinning, bow-legged guard as he beat some wretched prisoner lying there helpless in the glaring white dust. Indeed, he had been unable to stop Frenssen from pitching one Japanese, who had persistently kicked a dying Englishman with his heavy, cruelly-shod boot until he had finally died there, choking in his own blood, right into the scummy, oil-flecked water of the harbour. In the end, Christian had been glad when the Japanese naval authorities had given the U-82 permission to sail on the start of its first mission in the Indian Ocean…

Off Cap St Jacques, some thirteen kilometres downstream from Saigon, the men of the U-82 had been surprised to see another U-boat steering a slow course towards them, its sides crusted with salt and barnacles as if it had been at sea a long time. 'One of the U-50 class, sir,' Frenssen had announced, as he had focused his glasses on the strange U-boat, and then suddenly he had laughed out loud, the first time he had laughed so uproariously since they had met the Japanese. 'Why

… why,' he stuttered, 'it's old Trainburster Thomas! Great crap on the Christmas tree! I thought the Big Lion had beached him years ago!'

It *had* been 'Trainburster Thomas', famed throughout the U-boat Army for the fact that throughout his 'fighting' career in submarines, his total booty had been a Greek locomotive which he had knocked out with his cannon off the Greek coast back in 1940. Twice the Big Lion had beached him because of his lack of success, but had been forced to recall him due to the growing losses in U-boat skippers.

Now here he was in person, tall, miserable and stooped, the usual dewdrop hanging from his long red nose; for he always seemed to have a cold, winter and summer. Through the loudhailer, Christian had greeted him with a hearty, 'Well, shipmate, on patrol at last! How's the hunting?'

Trainburster Thomas had taken his time. First he had whipped the dewdrop from the end of his long nose; then he had adjusted his battered white cap worn in the style of the great U-boat aces; finally he had picked up his megaphone and answered, 'No such luck, shipmate. We're to deliver this one to the Japanese. The Führer's given 'em it as a present. They want to copy it. All I am, shipmate, is a frigging errand boy for the Big Lion!'

Expertly he had whipped yet another dewdrop from the end of his big nose and had stared enviously at the many white 'kills' painted on the side of the U-82.

Christian had taken pity on him. The poor bastard was a jinx. He had heard of more than one eager young officer forcing his way into the Big Lion's office to protest against being posted to Trainburster Thomas's ship. On board any submarine commanded by him, they knew there would be no glory to be earned. 'Perhaps after this one, they'll give you a combat command, shipmate,' he had cried encouragingly.

The other skipper had shaken his big head sadly. 'Not for me, shipmate. Once I've delivered this old tub, I return to Kiel, courtesy of the Spanish Merchant Marine. They couldn't even send a honest German ship to bring us home,' he had said bitterly. 'No, I have to sail back with the frigging spaghetti-eaters!'

'And then?' Christian had prompted, trying to repress his grin at the look on the other skipper's ugly long face.

'And then I set out all over again — to deliver the second sub the Führer has promised the Japanese. *Me, I'll be a frigging errand boy to the end of the frigging war!*' He had sighed like a man sorely tried, and cried, without too much enthusiasm, 'Good hunting, comrades!'

And with that Trainburster Thomas had sailed on to meet the Japanese pilot boat which would guide the U-boat into Saigon Harbour…

Now, as Christian Jungblut lay stretched out on the heaving raft, his tongue filling his parched mouth like a piece of shrunken leather, he envied Trainburster Thomas. Somewhere out there in the rolling blue sea, glittering in the rays of that cruel, relentless tropical sun, he would be safely established in some old Italian tub, drinking as much ice-cold beer as his skinny stomach could stand.

Slowly he began to drift off again into one of those hallucinations which had plagued him ever since the first day. A beautiful island in the middle of the ocean … palm trees casting cool shade … everything green, lush and damp… Native women, naked to the waist … and there in the middle, Trainburster Thomas, togged up as a native king sitting on a throne, drinking a huge stein of foaming, ice-cold beer … and every time that Christian reached out to take the stein, one of the half-naked native women would whack his outstretched arm with the great pole-fan with which she was fanning a grinning Trainburster Thomas.

Slowly great sad tears of self-pity began to trickle down Christian Jungblut's burnt face. Watching like a worried mother, Frenssen clutched the water can anxiously to his belly. If it didn't rain tonight and fill the damned thing, he knew the skipper wouldn't last a third day on the raft. Carefully, very carefully, he dipped a piece of kapok in the precious water, allowing it to absorb a few drops. Then he pressed the damp material to Christian's cracked and swollen lips.

The skipper began to suck the material greedily like a baby at its mother's nipple…

CHAPTER 3

On the same day that *Obermaat* Frenssen decided that his skipper would not survive another day on that little raft if he did not get water, eight thousand miles away, Private First Class Benjamin Washington Lee Junior made his own overwhelming decision about the future too. And once again, it was drinking water which brought the matter to a head…

'Kin I have me a drink, cap'n?' he asked the greasy cook hopefully, the sweat glistening on his dark face as he stood there humbly outside the door of the cook-house.

The cook turned slowly, as if it took a lot of effort to do so. His belly bulged beneath the greasy singlet he wore, and for some reason he had a forty-five pistol dangling from his belt. 'You speaking to me, boy?' he asked in the thick accents of the Deep South.

'Yessir, cap'n,' Lee answered. He beamed at the fat greasy cook hopefully, while the other American mustered him with pig-like, red-rimmed eyes. He saw the look in the cook's eyes and backed off. 'Just thought I'd ask for a drink o' water, cap'n, sir,' he said apologetically, playing the humble Uncle Tom that the white trash liked. Yet at the same time his initial fear was beginning to turn to rage. What gave the fat bastard the right to treat him like this? He was only a goddam Private, too. Besides, all he had asked for was a glass of goddam water!

The greasy cook was staring at him now with his hand on the butt of his big pistol. 'Is you one o' dese tough black guys, eh?' he demanded.

Lee swallowed hard. He didn't know what to say. He knew what the fat bastard of a cook wanted him to say. He wanted him to grovel and stutter, 'Nossuh, not me, sir, cap'n,' and roll his eyes like one of those black characters in the movies who always were scared of their own shadows, just like the white trash liked them to be.

There was a heavy silence broken only by the noise of the beans bubbling in the big cookpots and the muted sound of the Andrew Sisters belting out 'The Boogie-Woogie Bulge Boy of Company B' over at the barracks. It wasn't chow for another hour and Lee knew the mess hall would be empty. The other cooks and the guys on Kitchen Patrol would be playing poker in the back. He was all alone — at the mercy of this goddam redneck.

'Come here, boy,' the cook commanded, breaking the silence, his voice suddenly hoarse. 'D' ya hear — come here!' Slowly, very slowly, not taking his little pig-like eyes off the young man's handsome face for one moment, he began to draw the big pistol out of its leather holster.

'Why yo' want to go messin' around with me, cap'n?' he protested hoarsely. 'I dun want no trouble... I —'

'Come here, *boy*!' the cook hissed, the pistol levelled at Lee now, something akin to sexual lust glistening in his eyes.

Lee tottered a few paces forward, still clutching the mud-encrusted shovel.

The cook grinned coldly, as he raised the big glistening blue-black pistol even more. 'They tell me you black boys don't like it the way we white folks do it. They tell me,' he drawled, savouring the fear in the other man's face, 'that you black trash make love with your mouths — *and like it!*' With startling speed for such a fat man, he reached out his pudgy hand and grabbed Lee by his cropped hair.

'*Hey!*' he yelled with pain as the cook dragged him towards the pistol, which loomed so large that it seemed to fill the whole world. He was so close to it that he could smell the sickly odour of gun-oil and the linseed grease with which the cook had polished the butt.

For what seemed an age the cook held him there, the pistol pointing right at his open mouth, as he gasped with fear, feeling his limbs shaking as if he were in the throes of some tropical fever.

The cook licked his fat sensual lips and they gleamed a bright red. Saliva trickled down the corner of his unshaven chin. 'You like to eat it, boy?' he choked. '*Eh?*'

Lee tried to pull away, eyes screwed up with pain. But the cook didn't give him a chance. He tightened his grip on Lee's cropped hair.

Lee gritted his teeth together, face set stubbornly, the sweat pouring down his forehead now. He was damned if he was going to do what this crazy redneck wanted him to. Angrily the cook rammed the muzzle against Lee's lips — hard. He felt his upper lip split and his mouth filled with the copper taste of his own blood.

The cook cursed and took the pistol away from Lee's mouth, the muzzle now flushed with blood. Still gripping Lee's hair, he hissed (and now Lee could smell the stale stink of booze on his breath), 'Listen, boy, I'm not gonna ask you agen. *Now open yo—*'

Suddenly something broke inside the young black man. He had been taking this sort of crap ever since he had joined the goddam Army. He was going to take no more of it. Seized by a sudden fury, he wrenched himself free from the startled cook's grasp. Instinctively he raised the spade. Opposite him the cook staggered against the range, fumbling with his pistol. Lee knew what was going on in his mind. He was going to shoot him. Later he'd plead self-defence and the authorities would believe him. The white brass always supported its own kind. If he didn't act at once, he would be a dead man.

Almost instinctively, as the cook clicked off the safety catch and raised the Colt, he brought the spade down, *blade foremost*. It cleaved the cook's balding skull easily. One moment he was standing there, heavy pistol raised, ready to blast the pesky black into eternity; the next he was sagging limply against the stove, a great blood-red gash dug into his forehead, the pistol hanging from nerveless fingers. Slowly, very slowly, he started to sink to the floor of the kitchen, the blood jetting from his ruined head in a bright-scarlet arc; while Lee stared at him in wide-eyed horror.

He had killed a man… *A white man!*

On the stove the beans began to boil over, slithering and spitting in a white and red stream onto the red-hot metal, and from there, hissing like lava, they continued to spread out to right and left of the dead cook…

How long he remained standing there, listening to the splutter of the cascading beans, staring at the man he had just killed, Private First Class Benjamin Washington Lee Junior would never know. His mind was too full of the horror lying slumped on the floor in front of him, slowly being submerged in beans. His mind raced electrically. He knew he hadn't a chance if he surrendered himself to the authorities. They'd try him, of course, but they'd still string him up in the end. But what could he do? Black men stuck out like sore thumbs here in England. Where could he run to and for how long, with only twenty dollars in his back pocket? Suddenly it dawned upon him. There was only one chance left for a black man on the run. He had to get back to the States. There he could become the invisible man once again, for that is how he had always thought of himself in a white man's world. Again he'd be a negro, a no-good negro, who drifted through *their* world like a black ghost, his negro presence only acknowledged when some irate redneck decided he needed his 'goddam black negro ass' kicking off the sidewalk.

The shock vanished from his numbed face. His eyes flashed once more. Suddenly he was thinking again, reasoning, planning, his ears already aware of the sounds outside; the clinking of tin plates, the clatter of cutlery as the Kitchen Patrols started to lay the big trestle tables for the afternoon chow. Soon, too soon, they would be coming in here, asking for free coffee, trying to steal the franks from the big pans which went with the beans, while the cooks' backs were turned.

Time was running out. *Fast!* He swallowed hard and bent down. First he took the fat cook's billfold and then, as an afterthought, he pulled his pistol from between bean-sticky fingers. A moment later he was sauntering casually out of the kitchen, still carrying his shovel, as if he hadn't a care in the world.

Half an hour later, clad in his best uniform, freshly shaven and washed, he was standing outside the gate of the camp, raising his thumb every time a truck driven by a negro went by. White men never stopped for blacks.

He didn't have to wait long. The big fat corporal with a half-smoked cigar stuck behind his ears, who had Alabama written all over his glistening porker-face, jammed on his air brakes and opened the door of the deuce-and-a-half. 'All aboard, soldier,' he chortled.

'Yassuh,' Lee grinned back at him, telling himself his luck was magic after all.

'And where yo' going, son?' the corporal asked, slipping out the clutch and drowning the sudden noise now coming from the kitchen.

Lee grinned at his sweating reflection in the driving mirror, ignoring the noise and the men running out into the company street, waving their arms as if they were crazy, shouting and screaming. 'Me, Corporal? Why, I'm going to London to see the town, that's what I'm gonna do.'

'Sho nice for you, son,' the corporal said, and winked at him in the mirror knowingly. 'But if yo' is gonna get any o' that white meat, brother, yo' gonna need plenty o' dough, yes man!' He chuckled and his black heavy jowls waddled.

Lee winked back at him. 'I've got dough and then some. I can find me all the white meat I can manage.'

The corporal sighed. 'What you got in that AWOL bag of yourn?' he asked a little enviously, indicating the grip Lee was holding on his knee. 'A lot of goodies for the black market? Scotch?' He licked his fat lips as if in anticipation.

Lee shook his head and relaxed in his seat, as the truck gathered speed. 'Nossuh. No black market. No scotch. I just know something, that's all…'

The Corporal opened his mouth as if to say something, then he changed his mind and concentrated on driving along the narrow winding English road. Next to him Private First Class Benjamin Lee Washington Junior told himself he really *did* know something that should be worth money. He knew about Bigots…

CHAPTER 4

Now the gloom was beginning to pale. A spectral sickle moon was rising to starboard. The clouds parted and the curve of an icy disc hung there over the ocean, cold and unfeeling. Stubbornly Frenssen held on to his can, moving his head from side to side stiffly, eyeing the departing clouds, wondering if they were taking any rain that might fall with them.

Beside him on the gently swaying little raft the skipper had drifted off into an uneasy sleep once more, muttering to himself, almost angrily, occasionally gritting his teeth, tossing and turning, as if he might be in the grips of some particularly unpleasant nightmare.

Frenssen licked his parched lips with a tongue that felt like a piece of rough, dried-up leather and stared desperately at the swaying, plunging horizon. This was the third day now. If it didn't rain today, he knew, Jungblut would reach the end of his endurance. He'd die and it wouldn't be much longer before he, too, croaked. If only they could spot a ship, even an enemy one!

Frenssen fell into a kind of open-eyed doze. Sometimes he seemed to see shadows darker than the night. Ships? But no, just shadows. He let his mind wander. Beer … and yet more beer. He remembered those waterfront bars in Hamburg and around the *Reeperbahn*, where the cheerful, big-bosomed waitresses would serve great foaming half-litres of suds all day and all night long. In each big hand they would carry half a dozen steins. *Six whole litres of cool, delightful, delicious beer!* Almost sadly the big petty officer licked his lips at the thought. *Six litres…*

Probably he drifted off into a shallow doze then. For when he came to again, there was a kind of white mist stealing across the surface of the ocean and sailing soundlessly through the damp white clouds there came a dark shape, what appeared to be small lights flickering nervously along its length. Frenssen blinked rapidly. As an afterthought, he trailed his big hand in the cold ocean and wet his face with the seawater.

There was no denying it. Something ... something that looked very like a ship was approaching them on the starboard side. He swallowed hard, his throat like emery paper. Could it be...? Could it be they were saved?

Slowly, hardly daring to believe the evidence of his own eyes, not taking his gaze off the dark shape for one instant, he reached out his free hand and shook Jungblut. 'Sir,' he croaked urgently. 'Sir ... wake up...'

'Let me sleep!' Christian moaned. 'Please, let me sleep... It's been a hard, long watch... *Please*, let me sl —'

'Wake up, damn you!' Frenssen interrupted harshly, feeling new strength surge through his big body, strength engendered by hope.

'Oh, what is it?' Christian asked irritably, waking up at last. 'Where's the fire?'

'A *ship*, sir!' Frenssen breathed the magic word. 'There's a *ship* out there, sir!'

Slowly, very very slowly, Christian raised himself, as if every little movement needed a tremendous effort of willpower. 'You're seeing things, Frenssen,' he grunted, his swollen tongue seeming to fill his mouth, making his speech awkward and slurred. 'You're halluc —' He stopped dead. 'Oh, my God!' he gasped. 'You're right, Frenssen. *It is a ship!*'

Christian stared to his front in stunned disbelief. But it was true. Plodding steadily in their direction was an old tub of a freighter, obviously neutral for it was lit up the length of its deck and superstructure as in peacetime, and there was a spotlight playing on the large flag, which he couldn't quite make out, on her flaking rusty side. Whoever the ship's captain was, he was making sure that any prowling submarine skipper, whatever his nationality, knew that this ship didn't belong in the war.

For what later seemed an eternity, the two comrades stared in sheer bewilderment at the approaching ship, as if they could not quite comprehend what was happening. And then Christian woke up to the fact that the crew or lookouts might well miss them if they didn't do something to attract their attention. '*Quick!*' he hissed urgently, his fatigue forgotten, every nerve tingling electrically, adrenaline pumping new energy into his worn skinny body. 'Take off your clothes, Frenssen!' Without waiting for the other man to comply, he began ripping off his own tattered sun-bleached shirt and trousers, fumbling while he did so for his lighter, praying that the thing would work after being soaked when they had been sunk.

Puzzled, Frenssen did the same, dropping his pathetic rags in the centre of the little raft where the skipper had dropped his. Now totally naked, Christian said a quick prayer and flicked the wheel of the cheap Japanese lighter. *Nothing happened!*

'What you gonna do, sir?' Frenssen cried, as Christian tried again.

'Set fire to our duds, *to the shitting raft itself*, if it will burn! We've got to have a signal for them!' Frantically he clicked the wheel of the lighter once more with fingers that felt like thick, clumsy sausages.

Now the old tub seemed to fill the whole horizon. Even as he sweated over the stubborn lighter, Christian could make out the yellow, red and black of the Spanish flag painted on the ship's rust-flecked sides. His heart leapt. If the Spanish rescued them, it would mean that they wouldn't have to end the war in some damned prisoner-of-war camp into which neutrals usually put belligerents. General Franco, the Spanish dictator, was very pro-German. The Spaniards would ensure that any Germans who fell into their hands would be quietly returned to their own land. But first they had to be damned well rescued!

Frantically he clicked the wheel for the third time. A shower of blue sparks. But no flame. The ship was beginning to move by them. It was now or never.

'Light, damn you, *light*!' he cursed fervently and tried once more.

A sudden flame! Blue, weak and flickering. Carefully he guarded it against the faint wind. 'Give me your shirt, Frenssen,' he hissed, not taking his gaze off that faint swaying flame for one instant. '*Quick* — and pray to God that the shitting thing lights!'

Hastily Frenssen tendered him his ragged shirt, caked with oil-waste.

Praying frantically himself, Christian applied the flame to the shirt next to the caked oil. The thunder of the ship's engines was ear-splitting. Beneath them the raft started to sway wildly in the waves its screws kicked up. His nostrils were assailed by the stink of an old ship, a mixture of oil, sweat and stale cooking. His stomach churned.

Suddenly — delightfully — it happened. The shirt began to burn! The flame was weak at first, but gathered in strength by every second. Christian didn't hesitate. He bent down and applied the flaming shirt to the bundle of rags at his feet.

'Blow, Frenssen, for Chrissake — *blow!*' he commanded, panic in his broken voice now.

In a few moments the freighter would be by them and that would be that.

With surprising speed for such a big man, Frenssen flung himself down on his hands and knees, big naked rump stuck absurdly into the air, and began blowing at the flickering smouldering rags as if his life depended upon it, which it did.

The red embers grew in strength. A splutter of caked oil. Frenssen blew even harder.

'*More!*' Christian cried frantically.

The rags started to glow. Now there was a proper flame glowing a bright cherry-red.

Frenssen filled his lungs, his enormous chest swelling up like a balloon, and expelled a tremendous blast of air at the tiny flame. It exploded into a fierce scarlet. Abruptly they had a bonfire crackling and sparking madly in the middle of the crazily swaying raft and far, far above the two naked wretches an excited voice was crying suddenly, in a language they couldn't understand, but which at that moment was sheer music to their ears, '*Mire mire ... teniente ... un fuego!*'

Trainburster Thomas handed Christian yet another ice-cold beer, carefully wiping the dewdrop from the end of his long red nose before he did so, saying in those mournful tones of his, 'Heaven, arse and cloudburst, Christian, where are you putting all those suds? That's the third half-litre you've whipped behind yer collar in the last half hour. Captain Gomez is already complaining we're running out of beer.'

Christian took another deep, delightful draught before he answered, saying, 'Christ, Thomas, don't you realize I've got a hole in my stomach and my legs are hollow? I could go on drinking these suds till final victory — and then some!' He grinned up at the jinx of the submarine fleet, happy with the clean sheets, the fact that he could see again, and that he was going home, after all.

This time, at least, the sea wasn't going to have him.

Thomas muttered something in that slow, mournful manner of his and then said, 'Anyway, it's good to see you alive, Christian. The Japanese told us by radio that none of the U-82's crew had been saved.'

Christian's smile disappeared, as he thought of all those young men of his who would never see their homeland again, lost at sea — and for what? Just so the Big Lion could gain time in order to employ his new wonder weapons; that is, if such wonder weapons really did exist.

'Thomas,' he said slowly, as the ancient *Puerto de Barcelona* plodded steadily westwards, heading for the entrance to the Red Sea and from there home through the Mediterranean, 'you're based at Danzig and that's where the Big Lion tests his new equipment, away from prying eyes.'

Thomas nodded his big ugly head. 'Yes, so far neither the Ivan recce planes nor those of the Western air gangsters have managed to reach Danzig. It's just like a peacetime station, for those who like such things.' He sniffed miserably, as if he were remembering his own lack of combat experience.

Christian pointed his half empty glass almost accusingly at the other man supporting his emaciated body against the bulkhead. 'Thomas, I'd like to ask you something?'

'Fire away, old house.'

Up above them on deck, Frenssen, who was already fully recovered from their ordeal, was bawling away some shanty for the sake of the Spaniards who kept him plentifully supplied with the coarse powerful red wine that they preferred to beer.

Christian hesitated only an instant, before asking, 'Have you heard anything, Thomas, about a new class of submarines - *the Century Class*? The Big Lion himself mentioned them to me before he sent me off on that damn fool mission to Japan.'

Thomas took his time, but then he always took his time, and as Christian watched him wrinkle his forehead and purse his lips prior to answering, he told himself he wouldn't like to be Thomas's girlfriend. She'd have a terrible love life. By the time Thomas got his pants off, she wouldn't be interested any more. He swiftly repressed his grin at the vision of tall skinny Thomas without his trousers on.

'Heard of them, I haven't, Christian,' he answered slowly. 'But seen them, *I have* — out in the Bay of Danzig. And I've seen the new tin fish they're using, too,' he added with sudden animation in his dreary voice.

'New torpedoes?' Christian echoed.

'Yes. You don't need to aim those beauts. Set 'em off in the general direction of the ship you're attacking and no matter how violently the target ship tries to outmanoeuvre the tin fish, it always strikes home. Believe me, Christian, I've seen it work.'

Christian was impressed, but curious too. 'But what about this Century class?' he persisted. 'What do you know about them, Thomas?'

'Well, as I say, I've seen them out in the Bay and they don't look much different from most other U-boats, except there's something strange about their superstructure.'

'Strange?'

Thomas wrinkled his brow. 'Yes, but it's hard to put one's finger on what exactly is strange about it. They have always been too far away when I've seen the Century class. But one thing I can tell you, Christian, whether you believe it or not.'

'And what's that, Thomas?'

'The rumour in Danzig when I was last there was that this new class need never surface.' He saw the incredulous look on Christian's face and nodded his head vigorously. 'It's true, I tell you! When I was last there there was a rumour doing the rounds, that one of these Century class subs could sail round the whole world soon — *and never surface once!*'

Christian lowered his beer and whistled softly through his cracked lips, visibly impressed.

Above on the hot deck, Trainburster Thomas's crew had joined a drunken Frenssen in a hearty chorus of 'The Mate at the Wheel Had a Bloody Good Feel at the Girl I Left Behind Me', giving the song the full impact of their cynicism. All of them knew from bitter personal experience just how loyal the average U-boat sailor's girl was.' About forty-eight hours and as much time as it takes her to get her fornicating apparatus back in working order after Frau Frenssen's handsome son has had his wicked way with her,' as *Obermaat* Frenssen was wont to comment in his more reflective moments.

'A weapon like that,' Christian said carefully, thinking hard, 'could yet win the war for the Homeland. Imagine, when the Amis and Tommies start to cross the Channel for their vaunted Invasion, what a skipper could do with a craft like that. Invisible and armed with a tin fish that would find its target regardless of how badly it had been fired.' He slammed his free fist against the steel bulkhead, carried away by a sudden wild excitement. 'My God, Thomas, it would be mass slaughter! Given enough boats, we could send the whole damned Invasion fleet to the bottom of the sea, before one single enemy soldier had set his foot on French soil.'

Even Trainburster Thomas's long mournful face showed some animation now, his sunken cheeks suddenly flushed a hectic red. 'Do you really think so, Christian, *really*?' He leaned forward like a small child waiting to be told some well-beloved fairy tale.

'I don't just *think* so, you long streak of yellow piss!' Christian cried exuberantly, draining his beer in one swift, excited gulp, 'I frigging well *know* so! By the great whore of Buxtehude, where the dogs piss out of their ears, *we're gonna win this damned war after all…*'

CHAPTER 5

The morning was bright with winter sunshine. But the January sun had no warmth. Yet its rays gave the bomb-shattered buildings everywhere a mellow look, so that they fitted in with the rest of the capital, as if they had fallen down a long time ago.

Lee walked through the crowded streets purposefully, dark eyes always on the alert for Military Police, as if he had somewhere to go and something to do urgently. Everywhere there were service people; British, American, Australians, Frenchmen and half a dozen other nationalities which he could not place. Above, the barrage balloons sailed over London in the hard blue sky like silver slugs, and in every park he passed there were sandbagged dugouts with 3.7 anti-aircraft guns stretching their necks to the heavens. A lone fighter crawled round and round, dragging its startlingly white vapour trail behind it. In a way, Lee found it all exciting and beautiful. But he knew the excitement and beauty of London in this January of 1944 were not meant for him. This was a white man's war, not his. He had no cause to be excited by it. He swung into Piccadilly, slowing his pace a little as he walked to the Rainbow Corner Club. Here no one walked in a hurry, especially if they were a GI or a whore; and both types were everywhere. Some of the GIs were already drunk; perhaps, he told himself, they were still drunk from the night before. They propped themselves against the walls, chewing gum, Ike jackets flung open carelessly, overseas caps thrust to the backs of their cropped heads, eyeing the whores in calculated boredom, watching them as they bent in the too-short skirts they wore, gazes hardening a little as the material rode up to show the white naked flesh above the black nylons. In their pockets they fingered their loose change loudly, and the English whores grinned in a cynical tired way.

All this Lee took in out of the corner of his eye, but although at that moment he could have used a woman urgently, he knew he was simply asking for trouble if he tried to proposition one, even if she was a whore, in broad daylight. The goddam rednecks would lynch him from the nearest lamp post. Instead he walked into the Rainbow Club, its front decorated by large American flags, straightening his shoulders smartly as he passed the club-swinging, white helmeted MP standing there, chewing gum as a bored cow might chew the cud. The cop didn't even look at him. He was back in the 'land of the round doorknob', as the GIs called the States. He was the invisible man once again.

In the big ballroom to the right, decked out with paper flags and streamers, the ancient English cleaning ladies were sweeping out the trash from the previous evening's dance. One of them, a toothless crone with steel curlers sticking out from beneath her coloured headscarf, was holding up a pair of silken, frilly knickers for the entertainment of the others, crying, 'I bet this one lost more than her bloomers last night, ducks!' The others cackled lecherously, and Lee shook his head as he passed into the recreation area where American girls in smart sky-blue uniforms were already serving coffee and doughnuts to bored, hungover GIs.

As always, he had to wait till last, but it didn't worry him. He had plenty of time — and he was used to it. Finally one of the ugliest of the girls walked over to him and snapped in a surly, almost angry manner, although he judged she was from the north by her accent. 'Wanna doughnut and Java, soldier?'

He forced a humble smile and said, 'I sure do, ma'am. Thank you kindly.'

She poured him a cup from the big can she was holding, slopping the strong brown coffee down the side of the cup, and handed him a doughnut without another word. He kept on smiling and muttered to himself, 'I wouldn't fuck you, baby, if you was the last broad on the earth!'

His smile vanished, he walked to the big window, crisscrossed with brown paper strips to prevent it breaking in a bomb attack, and stared out a little moodily at the winter street. Behind him someone had put 'The One O'clock Jump' on the jukebox and in the window he could see the reflection of the ugly canteen worker doing a few steps of jive, heavy coffee pot in her hand. He told himself he still wouldn't fuck her. He gazed at the street, now packed with Londoners going to work; the men all in the same dress, almost as if it were a kind of uniform — shabby trench coat, bowler hat, gas mask slung over the shoulder, and, naturally, the furled umbrella, carried like a sword; the women — headscarves and high heels, too-short floral frocks and shabby coats that looked as if they dated from before the war. Even though it was January many of them were barelegged. No wonder the grinning GIs, lounging outside, dangled nylons in front of them as if this was the most precious gift in the world to give to a woman.

Lee took a sip of the coffee. It was good and he savoured it as he stood there pensively wondering what he should do next. Out there somewhere there was someone who would buy what he knew, buy it with enough money to take him back to the States. But *where* and *who*? That was the problem.

Lee frowned at his own image in the window, a handsome young black man wanted for murder who didn't know what to do next...

As usual he had been digging ditches with the rest of his company when the Top Brass had arrived. He'd recognized Eisenhower immediately, bald and monkey-mouthed, the smile he always had ready for movie audiences absent this day. Next to him was a little Britisher, face beneath the overlarge floppy black beret hard and hawk-like, the eyes sharp and penetrating. To Lee pausing to watch in his trench with the other blacks, he looked like a real mean bastard, whatever the papers said about him. But mean bastard or not, Montgomery, the Britisher, was the only one of the Top Brass to wave to the black service troops and they had waved back, whether he had meant the gesture sincerely or not.

Once again he had been the invisible man, as Eisenhower had stared around the little group of high-ranking officers before barking, 'You are all Bigots here, I guess?'

There had been a murmur of assent and Montgomery had rasped in that high-pitched upper class voice of his, having difficulty with his 'r's as usual, 'Weally, Ike, what a question! Most of us here have been planning the damned thing for two bloody years now, ye know!'

There had been a rumble of laughter, heavy, confident, well-fed laughter, and Eisenhower had given them the benefit of that famed ear-to-ear smile of his before saying, 'Well, here we're gonna house the Twenty-Ninth Infantry Division. They'll go in in support of the Big Red One — the First US Infantry Division, for the benefit of you Britishers. As all you Bigots know by now, the Big Red One will be in the first American wave…' And then the Top Brass had moved away and the first sergeant was bawling, 'All right, yo' men, get the lead out of yo' asses and start digging!' But even as he had dug his spade into the chalky English soil he had begun putting two and two together and coming up with answers. That is how he had figured out what 'Bigot' meant. Suddenly that cold December afternoon, with the leaden sky above the dark-green sea full of snow, he had realized he had discovered a secret, and a *damn big one at that*!

'Hello there, soldier,' the voice said, warm and winning, as he came clattering down the stairs of the club, past the lounging soldiers whistling at some British ATS and crying, '*She'll be wearing khaki bloomers when she comes*!'

He turned, a little startled. A limey was standing there, looking like all the limeys he had ever seen in London, dirty trench coat, bowler hat, umbrella, cardboard box, carrying his gas mask slung over his shoulder. There was nothing different about him save that he was a little smaller than the average and his eyes had an un-English twinkle in them, as he smiled winningly up at Lee. 'You speaking to me, sah?' he asked, a little bewildered at the Englishman's approach, wondering if the limey was queer. The guys said most of them were, that's why their broads went for Americans in such a big way.

'Yes, soldier,' the limey answered, his merry blue eyes sparkling even more. 'I thought you were looking a little down in the dumps. A little lost in the big city. I wondered whether you needed any help? Please don't misunderstand me,' he added hastily, seeing the sudden wary look in Lee's dark eyes. 'I am not a … er, hm, pimp. Nor am I any kind of sexual deviant. Just an ally, trying to be friendly. Could I show you London or buy you a drink or anything once the pubs…' The words died on his lips, as he saw the direction of Lee's gaze.

Two fat MPs, both well over six foot in their white-painted helmets, swinging clubs threateningly, as if they wouldn't hesitate a moment to use them, were beginning to check the passes of the GIs lounging outside the club. The little man's friendly smile vanished. He grabbed Lee's arm urgently. 'Let's take a tube!' he commanded. 'There's an underground station nearby.' He saw the look on Lee's face and hissed swiftly, '*Underground … subway*! We can be out of here in seconds. Come on, old boy, let's go!'

They fought their way through the crowd, past the touts setting up the spaces for the night. 'A place at Oxford Street'll go for as much as ten shillings,' Lee's new found friend explained. 'Oxford Street has got water and lavs, you see.'

Lee didn't, but it didn't matter. His brain was racing as they trudged up the stairs out of the tube — the escalators hadn't worked for years — past the fading slogans daubed by the communists back in '42, '*Second Front Now*', and the mass of patriotic posters exerting the war-weary Londoners to '*Salute the Soldier*,' '*Keep Mum*' and '*Lend to Defend the Right to Be Free*!'

The little limey — Smith, he called himself — wasn't as harmless as he seemed. He had realized as soon as he had seen the two MPs that Lee was in trouble and he had acted accordingly. But why should he chance getting himself in trouble with his own authorities to help a black soldier he had only gotten to know minutes before? *Why*?

'They're checking passes!' Smith's voice cut into his thoughts. Now it was no longer so gentle and English; now his voice was harsh and grating. 'Up there — look!'

Lee stared at the top of the escalator, above the heads of the crowded, jostling civilians. A group of MPs, British in their red caps and Americans in their white helmets, were pulling servicemen, whatever their nationality, out of the crowd, and examining their papers. Already they had collected a drunken Australian in a big side-hat and an undersized Britisher in the blue of the RAF, both of them looking decidedly unhappy.

'Deserters,' Smith hissed, 'they're looking for deserters!' He flashed Lee a look and the latter knew that the little limey had realized exactly who he was. Smith kept staring at him as if he expected something from him, as the crowd of civilians, shabby, weary, some of them still carrying blankets from the night before, advanced slowly towards the waiting MPs.

Lee took a chance. 'Can you help me?' he croaked. 'I've gone over the hill — *deserted!*' he added quickly when he saw the other man didn't understand. 'I'm on the run... Can you help me — *please?*'

Suddenly Smith grinned. 'Certainly I can help you,' he replied, very calm now and very self-assured, as if it didn't worry him in the least that there were half a dozen MPs waiting for them at the top of the escalator, 'If *you'll* help me later.'

'Help you ... sure I'll help you,' Lee agreed, wondering how the hell he could help the little limey. Perhaps he was a queer after all. Perhaps he wanted *that*. But anything was better than Master-Sergeant Wood's rope noose. 'In any way I can...'

'Right then, leave it to me, soldier.' Now the little limey was no longer meek and humble. There was iron purpose in his voice and his face was set and determined. There's a tunnel to the right, leading from here to King's Cross. When I say "go", run like hell. Now smile, black boy, *smile for all yer fucking worth!*' And now there was no mistaking the authority in his tone. The little limey was used to giving orders — and having them obeyed.

'Hey, Corp, have a heart,' the skinny cockney soldier just in front of them was beginning to whine, as the British redcap stared at his pay book, a look of arrogant contempt on his face. 'Me old woman was bombed out last week, ye see, and I couldn't return to barracks and leave the old bugger up the creek just like that, could I...' His voice trailed away as the redcap stared down at him superciliously from beneath the peaked cap, which hid his upper face, so that he seemed without eyes. 'You're on the trot, ain't ye, mate?' he barked harshly. Next to him the big American grunted, 'Got another one, Charlie?' For an instant he took his eyes off Lee, the next American soldier to appear at the head of the steps.

'Have a frigging heart, mate!' the cockney pleaded, while the MPs began to gather around the snivelling little man with curiosity. 'I ain't seen the old bugger for over a year. Bloke's got to have a bit o' the other every now and agen or he'll go blind from wanker's doom…'

Smith didn't hesitate. The situation was tailor-made for him. He heaved his skinny shoulder into the big rump of the fat woman just in front of him wearing men's boots, her arms cradling a paper bag. '*Hey, what the frigging hell is going on* —' she began, startled, and then she was falling forward, right into the arms of the surprised American MP, the bag bursting on the floor, spilling its contents everywhere.

In an instant all was noisy confusion. The snivelling little cockney reached up and punched the redcap neatly on the chin. Whistles shrilled. The cockney was running madly in his heavy-nailed boots. Someone bellowed an angry order. A woman screamed. A civilian cried, 'I'm a doctor of medicine … give her air!'

'Oh my Godfather,' a cockney voice exclaimed, '*she's gonna have a nipper here and frigging now*!'

'*GO!*' Smith bellowed above the racket. Next moment the two of them were pelting all-out, arms moving like pistons, down the dark, white-tiled tunnel which smelled of cat's piss and ancient lecheries, their breath coming in harsh, strained gasps, the sound of the shouting and the police whistles dying away rapidly behind them…

CHAPTER 6

Captain Gomez, dark, fat and worried, pointed to the dark smudge on the horizon. 'The Strait of Bab-el-Mandeb,' he said in the heavily accented German he had learned in these last four years as a blockade runner for the German *Kriegsmarine*. 'The southern gateway to the Red Sea.'

Thomas and Christian nodded their understanding. This was the point of danger. Here in the narrow sea, the British maintained a permanent naval patrol to check all traffic entering what was really a British lake.

'Over there — Africa!' Gomez continued, wiping the beads of sweat from his greasy face although the sun had already sunk beyond the horizon and the evening breeze was refreshingly cool. 'Desert and a few wandering tribesmen... No English patrols.' He wagged a dirty finger at the two U-boat officers to emphasize his point.

Down below on the now blacked-out deck, Frenssen was commanding gruffly, 'All right, you bunch of piss-pansies, let's get these boats loaded. The skipper ain't got all frigging night, yer know!'

Christian frowned. He didn't like Gomez's plan one bit, although apparently it had been worked out for him by the Big Lion's staff at his Mürwik headquarters. Armed only with pistols and machine pistols, the crew of Thomas's boat, plus himself and Frenssen, were to be put ashore on the African side of the Straits. There, while the *Puerto de Barcelona* ran the British gauntlet — Gomez had already assured them that the Royal Navy would not hesitate to stop his ship and search for contraband, although it was neutral — they would make their way along the coast for two days to the agreed-upon rendezvous, a spot beyond the city of Hodeida where Gomez would pick them up again. There were too many intangibles. What if the British, for some reason, took the *Puerto de Barcelona* into custody? What if the natives weren't so friendly as Gomez made out they were — with their hand-fire weapons they weren't going to be able to defend themselves for long? What if Gomez betrayed them?

The greasy-looking Spanish captain seemed to be able to read Christian's gloomy thoughts for he flashed the tall, blond German a gold-toothed smile and said, 'Never fear, Captain. I shall do my utmost to get you to Barcelona. After all, no bodies — no this.' He made a counting gesture with his dirty forefinger and thumb, little dark eyes glittering greedily, 'The consul will only pay me *on delivery*!'

Christian gave a wintry smile. 'Well, that is some consolation, I suppose. Now, how are we going to signal to you to let you know that we are at the rendezvous?'

Gomez shook his head. '*You* do not signal, *I* do. There will be English ships everywhere in the Straits. I do not want you to draw attention to yourselves, understand?'

Christian and Thomas nodded.

Down below Frenssen was barking, 'Now check your water bottles — and none of that Spanish red wine in them either. In this heat that kind of sauce'll addle yer frigging brains, that is, those of you lot o' shitehawks who've got frigging brains!'

Christian grinned in spite of his worries. Frenssen was running true to form. Undoubtedly his own water bottle would be filled to the top with crude Spanish firewater; he was not scared of having the sun fry *his* brains. 'All right, Captain,' he said with a note of finality in his voice. 'Then I suppose there's nothing for it. We'll have to go.'

Gomez nodded urgently as if he couldn't get rid of the U-boat men quickly enough and indicated the sudden silver glow to port. 'Perim Island,' he quavered. 'They've got a searchlight over there. They'll probably have English patrol boats lying just off the island, too.'

'We get the message, Captain… We get the message,' Christian said grimly. 'Come on, Thomas. I don't think our type is very much in demand at the moment.'

Gomez stretched out his hand urgently, the look of relief all too obvious on his face. 'Good luck,' he said hurriedly. 'See you in two days.'

Christian took the hand, then wished he hadn't. It was soft and wet with sweat. Gomez was terrified…

All three of the *Puerto de Barcelona's* boats leaked. So they had spent the night rowing and bailing, rowing and bailing. Now stiff and worn, the U-boat men watched as the bright red ball of the sun hung on the lip of the horizon, casting its full glowing hue over the flat wash of the sea, illuminating the barren brown land that was Africa.

None of them were impressed. Even Frenssen who, after venturing, 'I wonder if we gonna see any o' them black-wimmen running around with the tits showing?', decided scornfully, 'as far as Frau Frenssen's handsome son is concerned, they can give Africa back to the frigging baboons!'

Now Christian, in the lead boat, concerned himself with running it ashore safely. The surf was high and fast and it took all the U-boat men's strength, sapped by the long voyage out to Saigon, to keep it from being swamped by the waves. But they made it and began the hard slog of beaching the boat on the long, sloping shore. Christian waited till the other two boats, skippered by Frenssen and Thomas, had cleared the surf too, then he dropped over the side into the ankle-deep water and began to plod heavily towards the brilliant white sand, the sun already cutting his eyes like a sharp blade.

He didn't like what he saw. The land was barren and inhospitable, a fringe of coastal sand bordered by low baked hills, their only vegetation stunted bushes and some sort of camel thorn. And the heat away from the slight sea breeze was horrific. Suddenly he felt himself gasping for breath and in an instant his shorts and shirt were soaked black with sweat. 'Fuck Africa!' he muttered under his breath and plodded on, his eyes searching the sand in front of him carefully. But there was nothing there to indicate that any other human being had ever trodden it. Nothing but a few broken shells and little patches of oil-scum deposited from the tankers which had passed this way. At that particular moment, standing on the blazing hot beach, he felt as Robinson Crusoe must have felt when he was first stranded on his desert island, as if he were the last man alive in the world.

'Sir.'

He turned, feeling his clothes stick to his body unpleasantly. It was Frenssen, burdened by his Schmeisser, his face crimson and glazed with sweat, as if with Vaseline. 'Oh, it's you, Man Friday!' he exclaimed.

'*Man Friday*?' Frenssen expressed surprise. 'Who's he when he's at home, sir?'

Christian forced a grin. 'Literature, Frenssen, literature.'

'You mean dirty books, sir?' he asked cheekily, wiping the sweat from his face with the back of his hand.

'Forget it,' Christian said, realizing it was even an effort to crack jokes with the big petty officer. 'While the others are getting themselves sorted out under *Kapitänleutnant* Gotha —'

'So that's what his real name is,' Frenssen said.

Christian shot him a warning glance and said, 'We'll move up to that sandhill over yonder to port. It'll make a good lookout point. We can have a look-see at the terrain from there. Come on.'

Frenssen gave a mock groan. 'I joined the Navy, sir, to see the world, not to frigging well *walk* over it!' Christian ignored him.

But the view from the sandhill presented them with no evidence that this barren coastal strip was in any way inhabited. All they could see from their viewpoint was more and more barren hills, reaching to the horizon, devoid of any form of life, shimmering in little blue waves in the ever-increasing heat. Ruefully Christian concluded that the only danger that might present itself over the next two days until they contacted the *Puerto de Barcelona* once more would come from nature itself. It seemed that this remote corner of Africa was totally devoid of human beings. But for once, *Kapitäleutnant* Christian Jungblut was wrong...

Now the long column of sailors worked its way across the barren boulder-strewn ground, where every dip and hole was flattened to the eye by the almost perpendicular rays of a smouldering, copper ball of a sun. It was furnace-hot. In that tremendous heat the sand shimmered a crazy wavering blue. Not a breath of wind stirred, although the sea was only five hundred metres away to their right.

'*Khamsin*, I think they call it,' Thomas said wearily through cracked lips as he and Christian plodded on heavily at the head of the column, while Frenssen, already laden with three machine pistols from those of the rear-guard who couldn't carry them anymore, brought up the rear.

'*Khamsin* what?' Christian sighed, too exhausted to be interested. He needed every little bit of energy just to keep on walking.

'I've read about it, Christian. It's a wind that comes right from Central Africa … blows in over hundreds and hundreds of kilometres, being heated more and more the whole day. It's a killer,' he added miserably, and even here in this searing heat there was the usual dewdrop hanging from his long red nose.

'That you can say again,' Christian agreed.

They plodded on wearily. Now the heat increased in intensity, fanned by the wind. It was a harsh blistering heat that made one blink with shock, as if a great oven door had been flung open to release a fearsome blast of searingly hot air. And the wind was increasing steadily, the sinister low growl it made making it even more fearsome.

To the rear of the column, Frenssen groaned and shifted the machine pistols which were digging into his big shoulder. '*Himmel, Arsch und Wolkenbruch* … what an asshole of a country!' He shook his big cropped head ruefully. 'What a place!'

At eleven that morning, Christian ordered a break. But there was no shade and for the most part the men crouched apathetically where they had stopped, all spirit knocked out of them by that hellish heat. They did not even have the strength to eat their rations and the two officers, plus Frenssen, had supervised them with drawn pistols as they had sipped their precious water so that they wouldn't gulp the whole lot in one greedy go. Now the sky was the colour of wood smoke and the sun was like a copper coin seen dimly at the bottom of a dirty pond. Christian shuddered. They were in for a storm, he knew it.

One hour later, as they marched up, the sea to their right already invisible in the heat haze, it struck them in full force. Even as Christian yelled an order for every man to squat immediately and link arms with his neighbours, that tremendous wind hit them at a roaring, howling 100 kilometres an hour. It struck the startled, frightened sailors like a wall of razor-sharp stilettos with lethal ferocity. Sand particles hissed through their thin clothing. Their skin was rasped as if by emery paper. They opened their mouths to howl with pain. But the wind snatched their cries from them and they were left gasping frantically for air like stranded fish.

The *Khamsin* grew in ferocity; an evil banshee-like howl. It became ever and ever more difficult to breathe. Now they were gasping for breath like ancient asthmatics, their lungs creaking like stiff leathern bellows. Men disappeared in that howling, hellish fog. Desperately they hung on to their neighbours to left and right, feeling their sweaty frightened grips, but unable to see them anymore. Above their bent heads the unending threnody rose to an ever louder pitch. The damned wind had travelled a thousand kilometres across Africa to attack this miserable handful of white men and it was not going to be denied its victims.

Time and time again it battered them as if with a gigantic fist. More than once Christian almost lost the grip he had of Thomas's clenched fingers and gulped with fear at the thought he might be swept away from the rest. But somehow he clung on. Next to him he could just hear Thomas mumbling his prayers like some fearful schoolboy.

Once, for moments, that terrible killer wind let up. Christian forced his head up and wiped the sand from his yellow-caked face. For a fleeting moment he thought he saw something dark and moving outlined against that rolling wall of yellow. But it was more imagined than seen. Next instant the wind was on them again. Fearfully he lowered his head like some dumb animal bending its head tamely before the executioner.

With renewed force the *Khamsin* struck them again. The wind shrieked and wailed furiously across the face of the desert, battering the helpless men cowering there, as if some god on high had ordained that they should be wiped from the face of the earth because of their temerity in venturing into his brutal, burning kingdom…

As abruptly as it had begun, it ended. Within a matter of seconds, that terrible banshee-like howl was replaced by a soft, ever-decreasing dirge. Then it was gone altogether, leaving behind a loud-echoing silence.

For what seemed a long while, the sand-covered men crouched in the track didn't move. It was almost as if they could not believe the evidence of their own ears; that that killing wind was over at last!

Blinded, with arms outstretched like sightless men, they reached forward to pat and feel their yellow, encrusted bodies. Christian gouged sand from the hollows of his eyes, spitting out the harsh dry particles at the same time. He reached out a hand to his chest and swept the sand to left and right. He shook his head. Next to him, Thomas came up for air, gasping like an old miserable walrus. On any other occasion Christian would have laughed at the sight. But not now. He felt too exhausted, too miserable. He ran his tongue around his parched, chapped lips. A thick wet streak broke the yellow mask which covered the lower half of his face. Slowly, infinitely slowly, like a very old man, he rose painfully to his feet and stared at the transformed desert, its surface changed totally by that mad wind.

'Holy strawsack!' Frenssen stuttered from the rear of the column, looking like a yellow sand giant. 'I must have just eaten half of frigging Africa He stopped short, mouth gaping open like a village idiot and stared hard at something just behind Christian.

Involuntarily, mesmerized somehow by the look in the big petty officer's eyes, Christian turned too, to gaze in that direction. He gasped with sudden shock.

On the gleaming new yellow ridge formed by the wind, there lay a score of men, dressed in the ragged dirty-white robes of the desert Arabs, their moth-eaten camels tethered behind them, and each and every one of them was armed with a rifle, *all pointing at the trapped, startled sailors…!*

CHAPTER 7

Smith had been thirteen when the Black-and-Tans had murdered his father. There had been three of them, armed with heavy automatics, big, tough men in the Balmorals, all of them obviously veterans of the Western Front. His father had tried to lie at first. *No*, the little farm he rented from the English absentee landlord in County Down had not been used by the 'Movement'! *No*, wasn't he an Englishman himself, with a name like Smith; and a Protestant to boot! *Why should he help the damned Roman Candles terrorize ordinary, decent Ulster folk...?*

They hadn't believed him. For a while the three of them, all ex-officers, lured to the Six Provinces by the promise of money and adventure by the looks of them, had played with his father, asking the odd idle question, punching him in a sort of routine, non-vicious way. That was until they had found the whisky. Thereafter they had turned sadistic.

Now they had stripped the shirt off his work-worn, skinny yellow body. The 'gaspers', as they called them, appeared suddenly from silver cigarette cases, engraved with regimental badges, puffed into sudden, bright-glowing flame. Time and time again they had pressed them out on his father's body until he could take no more. He had told them what they had wanted, and hiding in the attic listening tensely to it all, his hand around the muzzle of 'Sparks' to keep him quiet, he had believed his father was going to get away with it. But that wasn't to be. At the door, the biggest of the three, a hulking young giant with a scarred, evil face, had turned and said pleasantly enough, 'Well, goodbye, Mr Smith, *Englishman and*

Protestant, and many thanks for your information. May God reward you, sir!'

As if by magic the big Mauser had appeared from the pocket of his gleaming black mackintosh. Eyes wide with horror, he had seen how his father had crouched on his knees, hands raised in the classic pose of supplication, stammering, pleading for mercy. But in the Ireland of 1919 there was no mercy. Almost casually the big Black-and-Tan had aimed and fired. The bullet, at such short range, had lifted his skinny old father clean off his feet. He was stone dead by the time he hit the kitchen floor again. The big Black-and-Tan had laughed...

Two days later, still red-faced and shaking, he had unwrapped the big Smith-and-Weston his father (now hastily buried behind the cowshed by the Movement) had kept hidden in the attic for an emergency and had gone out to kill the first English soldier he had met. But there had seemed so many of them, all big, tough, heavily armed, and totally alert.

In the end, he knew it had to be Wilf. Poor old Wilf from Bradford, old and heavily moustached, who had survived the trenches and who was now serving out the rest of his 'time', as he called it, guarding the local bridge, waiting for the day he could be demobbed and return to the 'old woman and the kids'. He had always liked Wilf and Wilf had liked him too, he knew. 'Remind me of me eldest, you do, John,' he was fond of saying. 'Mind you, son, he don't talk funny like you do. A proper Yorkshire tyke he is.' And he would pat him on the head and give him a bar of precious ration chocolate.

He had strolled almost casually to the bridge, waiting till the midday traffic had crossed, and Wilf had been lulled into a state of eye-blinking torpor by the usual heavy midday meal — 'me snap', as he called it. Wilf had smiled to see him and had placed his bayonetted rifle next to him in the sentry box.

'Allo, young un,' he had cried happily. 'What's brung you out on a wet —'

The words had died suddenly on his lips. He had spotted the big heavy revolver in the boy's skinny white fist. He had gulped and now he had been able to see the fear in the old man's faded eyes, above the bayonet scar the Prussian Guard had given him on the Somme. 'Now then, Johnnie, we can't —'

He had pressed the trigger. The revolver had leapt like a live thing in his hand. But he hadn't missed. Suddenly old Wilfs face had begun to drip down on to his chest like red molten wax. His knees had started to give as animal, unintelligible noises had commenced coming from that red pit of a mouth; and he had been running for his life, as if the Devil himself were after him, clutching the big pistol to his skinny chest desperately.

One day later he had changed that hated English name, which had always branded him as one of the oppressors. Overnight he became the Irish patriot Sean O'Kelly. The flight south had come next. It was safer down there. The Movement had taken care of him. He had celebrated the foundation of the Republic and railed against the traitors. He had helped as a fifteen-year-old to set Michael Collins up, the traitor, and had laughed when the others explained how he had died in the ambush.

But thereafter Ireland had become too hot for those of the Movement who had sworn to rid all Ireland of the English and were prepared to fight on. He had wanted to go to his uncle in Boston, but the Movement had other ideas for him. The Chief had explained how in the War the Germans had helped the Movement with arms, gold and men. Now Germany was admittedly a defeated country, but still it could help the Movement when the time came. Thus it was that as a fifteen and a half-year-old, equipped with old addresses and two large white English five pound notes (worth a fortune in inflation plagued Germany that year), Sean O'Kelly, who had once been known as John Smith in another life, set out to establish contact with the old allies in a broken Weimar Republic...

In a Hamburg where working men demanded their money each midday and wheeled the billions of marks they were paid for a morning's work in a barrow to the nearest baker's to buy a loaf of bread, he lived like a little prince at first. For the equivalent of a shilling a day he resided in the finest hotel, the *Atlantic*, overlooking the Alster, the port's inland sea, the porters bringing up women to his suite every night; society women, aristocrats, ready to pander to his every wish for a couple of pennies.

Speedily, as with all young people thrown into a society where few people spoke English, he learned German. It was not grammatical, but it was quick and fluent and it ensured that he began to realize that amidst all the decadence and breakdown of morality in this defeated starving country, there were still those who believed Germany had been stabbed in the back — *der Dolchstoss*, as they called it bitterly — and could one day be restored to its rightful glory.

Bit by bit Sean, or '*der Ire*,' as his many woman friends called him happily, gratefully (for he was unlike their own war-worn men in bed), began to forget the newly found pleasures of sex. He started to frequent more and more these hard-eyed bitter men in their shabby military greatcoats, devoid of the old badges of rank; men who had once commanded battalions, regiments, and who were now reduced to selling bootlaces at street corners and their medals to any Jewish pawnbroker foolish enough to want to buy them.

That year he first heard of a new rabble-rouser down in faraway Berlin, a fanatic named Hitler. He had started something which was called grandly 'the National Socialist German Workers' Party', *with a total of thirty-seven members in all!* His new found friends, those embittered veterans of the Great War, still living in the past, had laughed when Hitler's plot to take over the state had failed in 1923. Three years later they were joining his party in droves as the last hope of saving Germany from the coming communist takeover…

It was now, as a very mature and sexually experienced eighteen-year-old, that *der Ire* had first began to make the contacts that the Movement had sent him to Germany to make. Suddenly Hitler and his Party had money; rich industrialists, and not only in Germany, saw in the Austrian fanatic the only way of preventing the Weimar Republic, with mobs of right and left-wingers fighting pitched battles on the streets of every big city daily, of going the same way as Soviet Russia. Now Bohlen, the Bradford-born *Auslands-gauleiter*, the man responsible for Party affairs abroad, interested himself in the young Irishman. He was sent back to Ireland to establish the first contacts between what was now called the IRA and Germany.

Money and weapons began to flow to Ireland once more as they had done back in 1914 when Imperial Germany had backed the Irish revolutionary movement. But these new German fanatics wanted more. They wanted details of the English armaments industry, her coastal defences, anything that might be of use to a Germany seeking revenge for the defeat of 1918 and the disgrace of the Versailles Peace Treaty which had stolen from the Reich one fifth of its territory. Gradually, very gradually, as the twenties gave way to the thirties and Hitler finally came to power, Smith, as he had once been called and was now called again, at least on the forged passport the German Intelligence had given him, realized he was no longer working for the Movement; he was working for Germany. Now he was little better than a Nazi spy!

In 1943, after his second nervous breakdown in Eire, old Father Christmas had ordered him to Berlin to meet the head of the *Abwehr* personally. There, there had been the usual gala dinners, the congratulations, the telegram from the Führer, even the Iron Cross solemnly presented by some general whose name he had been unable to catch. It didn't matter anyway. He had been allowed to look at the bauble for a few moments, then it had been taken away from him and placed in the safe for 'safe-keeping till victory'; a remark which had made Father Christmas sniff somewhat contemptuously.

Finally Admiral Canaris, the cunning-eyed head of the *Abwehr*, known behind his back as 'Father Christmas' due to his shock of silver-white hair, had got down to business. 'Smith,' he had said in that soft, sly manner of his, stroking his pet dachshunds, 'let us be realistic about things. Now that the Russians have gained the advantage — *temporarily* — in the East, Churchill, that drunken sot, will be forced to show his hand, to make some contribution to the war. Against his better judgment, he will be forced to invade Europe.' Canaris had fixed him with that piercing gaze of his. 'I should like to ask you to do one more — *one last* — mission for us before you ... *retire!*' He had smiled fleetingly. 'And retire a very rich man, I must add, courtesy of the *Reichsbank*, in any currency you wish. *Argentinian pesos*, if necessary!'

Smith had got the message. Canaris no longer believed in final victory. He was hinting that any smart agent should now be making plans to abandon the sinking ship before it was too late. 'What kind of mission, sir?' he had asked warily.

'*The Invasion*!' Canaris had answered simply, taking his gaze off the Irishman to watch as one of the dachshunds waddled over to the nearest chair and urinated.

'But that is a tremendous task, sir!' he had exploded. 'How can one man find out what the Anglo-Americans intend?'

Canaris had shown no emotion at his outburst. Instead he had said quietly, 'In essence, it is very simple, Smith. According to our calculations here in Berlin, the Anglo-Americans have sufficient strength to launch *one* single attack. The question which occupies our — er — beloved Führer,' he had looked away hurriedly, as if somehow he was suddenly embarrassed, 'is *where* that one attack will come. Now we have a huge coastline to defend. Hence all we can do is to discover where the mass of the assault force is located on the English coast and make our calculations accordingly.'

'I don't quite follow you, sir,' he had said.

'Well let us look at it like this,' Canaris had answered patiently, while his dark-skinned servant glided in noisily (some said he was Father Christmas's lover) and began to mop up the mess made by the dachshund, 'our High Command has decided that the Anglo-American Invasion will come at one of two points, Calais or Normandy. Von Rundstedt, the old fox, favours Calais. Rommel and the Führer think it will be Normandy. Now according to aerial reconnaissance, the Anglo-Americans have assembled their armies along the whole length of the English coast,' he moved to the big wall, 'from here in Kent right down to — here — in Devon. Here in Kent, we know that their General Patton has taken over command of an army, while in Devon their General Bradley is in command. So far, it seems as if Calais is going to be the spot where they will attack with Patton in charge. After all he lead their assaults on North Africa and Sicily. But can we be sure,

Smith, can we?' He looked hard at Smith with those dark unfathomable eyes of his. 'What if we put all our eggs in one basket and concentrate all our defences at Calais only to find they attack in Normandy? It would be a terrible defeat for German arms and mean the end of Germany.' He had nodded his white head gravely. 'Yes, Smith, there are no two ways about it. Germany will win or lose on those damned French beaches!'

'So my job then, sir,' he had said, 'is to find out which one of those two armies is the one which will carry out the assault?'

'Exactly.'

'If it's Patton's, then Calais is the target.'

'Yes, and if it's Bradley's, then Normandy is going to be the place where they'll land. It is as simple as that, Smith.' Father Christmas had forced a wry grin. 'In essence, my dear Smith, *the fate of the Third Reich is in your hands…!*'

CHAPTER 8

That fateful meeting with Father Christmas had been in October 1943. Now, three months later, Smith had got little further with his researches. He had discovered that the troops who were going to make the great assault were being trained at Burghead in the Moray Firth and Slapton Sands in Devon. Presumably there the beaches resembled the real ones they were going to attack one day soon in France.

But what little he had been able to squeeze out of the men practising those assaults, while they had still been allowed to go on leave to London, had brought him no nearer to the answer to the riddle. The few drunken infantrymen he had managed to pump in the bars around Rainbow Corner had told him the maps and photos of the real beaches they had been ordered to study bore only the code-names of their objectives; and only a few select officers knew what those code-names represented. Naturally none of those ordinary infantrymen, who might soon die in France, was in possession of such a map or photo so he might compare it with a map of France and discover the real location of the attack.

Nor had Smith been able to penetrate the coastal area itself in order to discover which of the two armies, Patton's or Bradley's, was fake. As 1943 had given way to that year of destiny, 1944, the whole of southern England had become one great armed camp, sealed off by a cordon of MPs and policemen from the rest of the country. Men and material, he had observed, streamed daily into the great camps established there, but none were allowed out again. Even the local civilians who had been permitted to stay in their homes there were now forbidden to leave. Even their mail had been stopped. 'American-Occupied England,' it was rumoured they now called their part of the country.

Allied Intelligence had established a second line of defence against any leakage of the great secret, too. Against long established diplomatic custom, all neutral embassies had been forbidden to communicate with their home countries. In particular, Eire's representatives in London were under the strictest supervision because of the flourishing German embassy in Dublin. Smith guessed soon they'd stop all travel between England and Southern Ireland. Then he would be trapped in London, and time was running out rapidly for him. Anyone who spoke with an Irish accent these days was automatically suspect in a London which swarmed with counter-intelligence agents and the men of the Special Branch. He could not last much longer. If he was to escape the disaster to come and collect that money Father Christmas had promised him, he had to discover which of the two armies was going to make the great assault — *soon*. If he didn't, he knew, the English would arrest him sooner or later and in England in this year of 1944, the English were no longer their customary hypocritical, mealy-mouthed selves. *In 1944 the English were hanging spies!*

Smith pushed the precious bottle of whisky — it had cost all of five pounds on the black market — towards the black man. 'Help yourself,' he said. 'There's water in that tin mug next to your elbow.'

'Thank you,' Lee grunted and took a look at the mug as if he expected it to be dirty inside. It *was*, like all the rest of the cluttered bed-sitter in which the limey, if that was what he was, lived. He contented himself with pouring a small shot of the scotch; he could do without the water. Smith noticed and smiled, as he unscrewed his bottle of pale ale — even on the black market these days you couldn't get a bottle of his favourite Guinness. 'Bit sloppy aren't I? But you know what bachelors are like.'

Lee answered his smile warily, noticing that the walls were plastered with 'crotch art', as the GIs called it — pornographic pictures, torn from magazines, of naked women with their legs spread. It was a good sign. Perhaps the limey wasn't a homosexual after all. He took a careful sip of the scotch.

'You stationed down in the south?' Smith asked, apparently casually.

Lee nodded. 'Yeah, in Weymouth.'

Smith affected surprise. 'But that's in the restricted area. How did … you manage it?'

Lee put down his glass. 'Listen buddy,' he said, feeling with his free hand the.45 tucked down the inside of his right leg, 'you know as well as I do that I've gone over the hill.' He saw the puzzled look on the other man's pale tormented face and explained hastily. 'Deserted! So quit fooling around. Why did you help me? Why did you bring me here?'

Smith hesitated. He had never had any dealings with black men before. He knew from his talks with other Americans that, at least in the US Army, they were regarded as third class citizens. Was it possible that their Intelligence authorities might use blacks for counter-intelligence purposes? 'I just wanted to help one of our boys who will be soon over there fighting against the damned Jerries.'

Lee put down his glass on the littered, stained table — hard. 'Cut out the crap, mister!' he snapped bitterly, dark eyes flashing. 'Black men in Uncle Sam's army don't fight... *We shovel shit*, that's what we do! So don't try to bullshit me. Now what's the deal?'

Smith hesitated still. Far away the sirens were beginning to sound their urgent warning yet once again. It was going to be another of these new tip-and-run raids, he guessed. Already he could hear the faint, muted thump of the ack-ack guns on the other side of the Thames. Carefully, very carefully, he phrased his words, knowing that he was committing himself irrevocably now. 'Perhaps,' he said, 'if you could help me,' he shrugged, as if it were all very unimportant, although his heart was now thumping away like a trip-hammer, '*I* could help you.'

Lee stared at him. 'How could I help you, mister?' he asked, as the wail of the sirens came closer and closer.

'With a little bit of information,' Smith answered softly, lowering his gaze so that the man couldn't see the look of fear in his eyes.

'What kind of information?'

'Oh, about this or that,' Smith said airily and took a hasty drink of the gassy pale ale. He belched.

'Piss or get off 'n the pot, mister!' Lee snapped crudely. 'You some kind o' spy or something?' He let his hand rest on the butt of the pistol beneath the tight smooth olive drab cloth. It was a comforting feeling. Now he knew where he stood. Perhaps he'd be able to make it back to the 'land of the round door knob' after all.

'I wouldn't say that,' Smith answered hastily. That word 'spy' had cut into him like a very sharp knife. 'I'm a patriot, in a way. You see I am not an Englishman, as you might think. I'm Irish and my government, although it's neutral, would like to know what's going on over here. It would help them to form their policy towards Nazi Germany. Why, Eire might even enter the war on America's side. After all a lot of our Irish boys are already serving in your army and the British Army as well.'

'Fuck your Irish boys!' Lee sneered. 'Irish or not, they're all white trash to me. Now mister, let me tell you what *I* want before —'

There was a tremendous roar which drowned his words. As one, their gazes flashed to the dirty window. A dark shape, with that familiar white and black cross clearly visible on its side, was hurtling across the shell-pocked sky outside almost at roof-top height. Behind, a Spitfire roared into the kill at four hundred miles an hour, its eight machine guns spitting lethal tracer. For an instant they were there and then were gone, that great ear-splitting roar vanishing with them.

Lee shook his head, took a drink and tried again, realizing even more urgently now that he had to get out of England and get out of it soon. For him, just as for Smith (though he didn't know it at that moment) time was running out fast. 'Now listen, mister, this is the deal. I'm a deserter and I ain't got a chance in hell if I stay here long. And brother, I don't aim to spend the rest of ma life in a stockade or Leavenworth. *I wanna live!* So what can I do? I can get back to the States and take a dive, that's what I can do. But how?' He looked hard at Smith. 'You say this Ireland place of yourn is neutral?'

'Yes.'

'Well, could a guy get a ship from there to the States?'

'Certainly. Ships are still running from Cobh to New York. There are some problems with the British, but it works.'

The room shuddered suddenly as the German fighter-bomber hit the ground a quarter of a mile away and exploded. Hastily Smith grabbed for the precious bottle of whisky, as it trembled and threatened to overturn on the table.

Lee didn't seem to notice. He bit his bottom lip, eyes vacant, as if his thoughts were far, far away.

Smith watched him, still holding the bottle. Was he going to be of any use, he asked himself. What would — *what could* — a black soldier know, who had confessed himself that he was only a 'shit-shoveler'? Was the black American worth investing time and money in? Of course, he could arrange a passage for him on the ferry to Southern Ireland. He could even provide him with fake papers. That was no problem. His old friends in the Movement could soon supply him with a British identification card for the American. But a black man with a National Identity Card would stick out at the ferry port like a sore thumb. The Special Branch there would twig him immediately. Slowly, very slowly, as the American slumped there, wrapped up in a cocoon of his own thoughts, Smith realized that even if the American could provide him with something, he'd have to get rid of him somehow. Should he turn him over to the American military police afterwards? No, that would be stupid. They'd be bound to ask questions and those questions would lead straight back to him. No, there was going to be only one way to deal with the black man…

'I know a military secret,' Lee broke into his thoughts with startling suddenness so that he jumped a little.

'What did you say?' he gasped.

'I know a military secret. I know something *big*,' Lee hissed, voice suddenly very low and tense. 'It's something to do with the Invasion… Something to do with the guys who know the score … where it's going to be and all that kind o' crap.'

Smith's mouth fell open stupidly. 'Do you mean to say,' he stuttered, 'that *you* know that?'

'Yeah.'

'But —'

'No buts,' Lee interrupted him harshly, feeling that comforting hardness of the .45 on his leg, knowing that he was the master of the situation. Now the white trash was listening to *him*, the negro, for a damned change. 'Get me a suit of civvy duds, enough dough in dollars, American, none o' that limey folding money, and a passage to the States, and I'll tell you what I know, Whitey — and I can tell you this now, it's real big!'

Smith sat there, still clutching the bottle of whisky, as if stunned. Outside, the sirens were beginning to wail once more, sounding the 'all clear'. The hit-and-run raiders had gone again, for a while. Now as the black man, apparently complete master of the situation, reached over, calmly took the precious bottle from his hands and poured himself a drink, Smith knew what he was going to have to do. The Negro was going to die. There was no other way. Just like poor old Wilf from Bradford all those years ago, he would have to kill a man again…

CHAPTER 9

Now the sun started to fade at last. Dark shadows, like sinister giant birds, began to race across the surface of the desert. Almost at once that horrific heat diminished. Christian breathed a sigh of relief and wiped the sweat from his flushed, angry face. 'Thank God!' he breathed to no one in particular, as somewhere a rifle fired and another slug whacked into the heap of sand that they had scraped with their bare hands to form a primitive wall. The boy who had been hit in the stomach moaned piteously yet again and in his delirium he called out for a mother he would never see again. Tenderly, Petty Officer Frenssen wet the rag with a few drops of the precious water and dabbed the dying youth's cracked and swollen lips.

Christian frowned. If they didn't make a break this night, they'd never make the rendezvous with the *Puerto de Barcelona* in time and, money or no money, he had an uneasy feeling that Captain Gomez would not wait another day for them. Besides, he knew his under-armed men, their water already virtually gone, could not stand much more of this terrific heat in the exposed desert.

On his hands and knees, followed by Frenssen's attentive, worried gaze, he crawled to where Thomas commanded the left flank. Even in this heat the other skipper's nose was still red and dripping. For an instant, Christian wondered how the devil he had ever got through the medical board for the submarine service with his health. 'Problems?' he asked, exhausted and sweat-lathered with the effort of crawling.

Thomas answered him brightly, as if this ambush in this remote corner of Africa was all great fun. 'No, not a thing. My fellows are doing exceedingly well for greenhorns. I reckon we must have bagged half a dozen of the black bastards. Look over there.' He raised his head above the sand wall and next instant a slug slammed into it only millimetres from where he crouched.

'Get yer damn fool turnip down, Thomas!' Christian cried urgently and pulled him behind the cover. 'That's not fried sausage they're throwing at us, you know. That stuff'll kill you!'

Thomas's eyes gleamed excitedly. 'But this is real combat, Christian! Five years in the U-boat arm and my real combat experience begins on land. Now what do you say to that?'

'Shut up, that's what I say!' Christian snapped angrily. 'Now stop the horse-shit and listen to me. Somehow or other we've got to break out of here as soon as it gets dark and make a run for it, or else tomorrow…' He didn't finish his sentence. Instead he pointed to the vultures steadily circling their positions overhead, attracted to the site of the little battle by the stench coming from the rotting camel which the sailors had shot when the Arabs or whatever they were had charged them.

Thomas swallowed hard, the dewdrop trembling at the bottom of his long nose. 'I hadn't thought of it like that, Christian. But how in three devils' name are we going to outrun them? After all, they have got those damned ships of the deserts.'

'The what?'

'Camels… It's a poetic image for a camel, Christian,' Thomas said earnestly. 'Have you never heard of it?'

In spite of his tense mood, Christian grinned wryly. 'Thomas, you are a frigging card, that you are! Listen, I've already thought of that. If you'll take care of the main party, I and that big rogue Frenssen will take care of their — ships of the desert. We'll nobble the ugly sods somehow or other.'

'Agreed, Christian. But there is only one thing.'

'What's that?'

'Leading Hand Salms.'

'You mean the one wounded in the guts?'

'Yes, Christian. What are we going to do about him? We can't take him with us, that is clear, isn't it?'

Christian nodded gloomily. 'Yes, you're right there, Thomas,' he agreed. 'He'd only spoil the chances of the others getting away.' He flashed a glance to where Frenssen tended the dying submariner and said, 'Let's hope he dies in time.'

'And if he doesn't?'

'Let that be my worry, Thomas. Now then, keep your turnip and ass down and start organizing your men.' Christian looked at the red ball of the sun, hanging now on the horizon, as if it did not want to depart. 'We move out in an hour's time, close to the sea. If the worst comes to the worst, we'll swim for it. I doubt if those Arabs can swim. Most of them look as if they had never washed in their lives.'

Thomas flashed him an excited grin, his dying seaman forgotten momentarily. 'Great crap on the Christmas tree, Christian, combat is really as good as having a woman, isn't it?'

'Give me the gash any time,' Christian said sombrely and began to crawl back to where Frenssen knelt...

Somewhere a wild dog or jackal howled at the sickle moon, which spread its cold, unfeeling light over the desert. Otherwise all was silent in the Arab camp. But the tense, waiting men knew they were still there all right. There was no mistaking that sweet, raunchy stink of their camels, mingled with the perfume of the green herbal tea they drank. Softly the dying boy began to moan once again.

Christian frowned and tried to listen only to the singing of the sand. Millions of sand-grains contracted in the cool of the night and now moving, rubbing against one another and giving out a strange, haunting melody. But he couldn't. All he could hear was the boy who was going to have to die here — alone — in this cruel, alien world.

'All ready, Christian,' Thomas broke into his reverie. 'We're ready to move out when you give the signal.'

'Good. I'll see to the wounded man first, Thomas.'

Thomas saw the look on the other officer's face and he whispered, 'He's my crew, Christian, I'll deal with —'

'No!' Christian cut him off harshly, mouth set and bitter. 'I'm senior man. It's my job. Then we're off to nobble the camels.' Shoulders bent, as if in defeat, he stumped through the deep sand to where the wounded man lay in a hollow, his shattered stomach packed in blood-stained bandages. 'Leading Hand Salms,' he said softly, staring down at the sailor's ashen, tormented face.

Slowly the boy's eyelids flickered and opened. 'Hello, sir,' he said weakly, recognizing Christian.

Christian knelt down behind him, pistol in his hand now. Salms's gaze fell on it and he nodded his head as if he approved. Christian frowned. He couldn't even do *that* for the poor wretch. 'I'm sorry, Salms,' he said gently. 'I can't do that … I can't shoot you. The Arabs would hear.'

'You're taking me with…' The sudden hope in the dying youth's voice vanished almost as soon as it had appeared. 'But of course you can't, sir, can you?'

Christian shook his head sadly. 'I'm afraid we can't, Salms. We're going to have to leave you here. You'll have to … well,

77

you know, when we've gone...' His voice trailed away to nothing, as he rose once more.

Salms looked up at him, standing there in the cold silver light of the moon and attempted to smile. 'Good luck, sir ... good luck ... and give my regards to the Homeland when you get back...' He coughed thinly and blood trickled out of the side of his mouth. Christian could have broken down and wept...

They crouched at the bottom of the long ridge, its side covered with stunted grass and camel thorn. Christian looked around at the young faces, a mixture of fear and excitement. 'Now listen, no one is to move until you hear the camels stampede and then it's off at the double! Anyone who falls out gets left behind. It's my guess' — Christian said a quick prayer that he was right — 'that they'll be too concerned about their frigging camels to bother about us. For a while. All right we're off — and Thomas.'

'Christian?'

'Don't wait for us. We'll catch up with you later.'

'Famous last frigging words,' Frenssen echoed dourly and slung his machine pistol more comfortably on his big back.

'Weeds never die, *Obermaat*,' Christian said unfeelingly. 'Now come on, you big rogue, let's get on with it.'

Digging their toes in the loose shifting sand of the height, the two men started the ascent. Millimetre by millimetre they edged their way upwards, nerves tingling electrically, ears tensed for the first suspicious sound. Within minutes they were soaked in sweat in spite of the coldness of the desert night. The sweat-drops trickled down their foreheads and threatened to blind them, so every now and again they had to toss their heads from side to side, like horses plagued by flies.

Now they were crawling through the murderous camel thorn. It tore and ripped at their flesh. Once Christian found himself caught by the damned stuff. Desperately, trying to make as little noise as possible, he twisted and turned until finally he had released the barbs which were biting into his flesh.

They crawled on, the thorn lashing at their sweat-glazed faces cruelly, tearing the flesh at a dozen spots. Time and time again the two men just prevented themselves from crying out in agony in time.

Then they had made it and were crouching there, gasping for breath, hearts thumping crazily as if they had just run a great race. Before them squatting in the sand were the camels, preposterous ugly creatures that, Christian could not help thinking, must have been one of God's jokes when He had created the world. 'You ready, Frenssen?' he whispered, trying to control his breathing.

'Ready as I ever will be, sir.' There was a dull gleam and Christian saw the big petty officer slip something on to his right hand.

'What's that?'

'The Waterfront Equalizer ... *brass knuckles* to you, sir,' he added grimly, holding up a fist like a small steam shovel. 'Just in frigging case.'

Christian nodded his approval. 'All right, off we go. You take the bunch from the left and I'll do the same from the right. We'll release the ones closest to the Arabs first, working outwards. Once we've undone the hobbles, yell like hell and then take your legs under yer arms and run for all yer worth!'

'Yessir,' Frenssen said and then with an almost casual nod to the skipper he began to crawl forward towards the ugly beasts. A moment's hesitation and Christian began to do the same.

Frenssen saw the guard just in time. There he squatted close to the ugly beasts, huddled together like a bundle of old rags, long ancient rifle resting on his shoulder. Perhaps he was asleep, the big petty officer told himself. But he wouldn't be for long. The camels were already beginning to shuffle uneasily, as they scented the presence of a stranger, raising their long awkward heads and looking to and fro.

'Mustn't like my frigging after-shave!' Frenssen whispered to himself and prepared for action, as slowly the bundle of rags began to come to life, obviously alerted by the camels' unease.

Frenssen crawled forward noiselessly, head down, big bottom raised in the air. The nearest camel stirred and Frenssen felt something warm and wet strike his left check. The whoreson had thrown a spit-ball or something at him, he told himself angrily, as he prepared to attack. The bundle of rags was already beginning to unsling his rifle. For the moment his gestures and movements were unhurried. Perhaps he thought it was some jackal or wild dog which was causing the camels to stir. But in a minute it would be different. He'd spot the figure crawling towards him and all hell would be let loose.

Frenssen took a deep breath. Next instant he dived forward. His heavy shoulder caught the Arab in his skinny chest. He hurtled backwards, a cry of alarm dying on his lips, rifle dropping from suddenly nerveless fingers. Frenssen didn't give him chance to recover. He lashed out with those cruelly armoured knuckles of his — *and missed!*

Agilely the Arab wriggled to one side and, as Frenssen blundered forward, he slid his two fingers into the German's nostrils — and pulled hard.

Frenssen bit his teeth into his bottom lip to stop the scream of absolute agony which welled up from his throat. The blood flooded his mouth. Tearing with all his strength, the Arab chuckled in triumph at Frenssen's contorted, agonized face beneath him.

Not for long. Instinctively Frenssen brought up his big knee. It caught the Arab solidly in the crotch. He choked and gagged, rolling away, as he swayed back and forth holding his savaged testicles. For one long moment Frenssen just lay there, nose and mouth full of blood and burning with pain. Then he lunged forward. Next instant his tremendous hands had wrapped themselves around the Arab's skinny neck. Knees spread apart, eyes bulging out of their sockets like those of a madman, veins rippling at his temples, Frenssen exerted all his gigantic strength. The Arab thrashed and gasped. Desperately he wriggled and twisted, trying to break that killing grip. To no avail! Frenssen held on grimly, his breath coming in short, hectic gasps. The Arab's struggles grew weaker and weaker. Suddenly his body went limp and he hung there in Frenssen's arms lifelessly, like a spent lover. Still Frenssen held on. He was taking no chances. For what seemed a long time the two of them clung together thus until finally Christian appeared out of the silver gloom, knife in hand.

'What in three devils' name…' he began and stopped short when he saw the dead Arab.

Frenssen shook his big head, as if waking from a deep sleep. Wordlessly and very gently he lowered the Arab to the ground. Silently, as if it were better not to speak, the two of them started cutting the remaining camels' hobbles…

'*Now!*' Christian hissed and slapped the nearest camel across its skinny, moth-eaten rump. Nothing happened. The ugly beast did not move. Instead it stared down at Christian in its stupid way, as if wondering what the devil this silly human being was doing waking him at this time of night.

'Leave the friggers to me, sir,' Frenssen snapped grimly, his spirit recovered now. 'Get ready to run.' He raised his Schmeisser to the cold unfeeling silver sky. *'Here we go!'* Without another moment's hesitation, he pressed the trigger.

The machine pistol chattered into wild frenetic life. At once the camels panicked. Suddenly they were running awkwardly in every direction, snorting in fury and fear, long skinny legs taking tremendous strides.

In an instant all was wild confusion. From the Arabs' camp there came an angry roar. Below, nearer the sea, Christian could hear the sound of men running. That was Thomas with his crew. He whipped out his own pistol as already wild streaks of scarlet flame stabbed the silver gloom. 'Come on Frenssen, let's leg it! *Dalli … dalli…!*'

'Dalli it is, sir!' Frenssen agreed hastily and abruptly they were running for all they were worth, weapons spitting fire as the Arabs spread out, caught completely by surprise, not knowing whether they were being attacked, or robbed of their precious camels, or both.

Minutes later they were through and the wild cries and shouts of anger were already beginning to die away behind them. They slowed down to a lung-gasping trot and finally to a walk.

Now that heavy hissing silence fell over the desert once more, broken only by one single shot far, far behind them. Frenssen gave Christian an inquiring glance. But the skipper kept his face set stubbornly to his front, his hard features revealing nothing.

'Poor young bastard,' Frenssen said softly, almost as if to himself. Then he forgot Leading Hand Salms, dead and alone in that remote place, and concentrated on the long march ahead…

CHAPTER 10

'*When that man is dead and gone,*' the sailor sang softly, cap pushed to the back of his head, face flushed with beer, '*some fine day the news will flash. Satan with a small moustache is asleep beneath the lawn... When that man is dead and gone...*'

Out of the corner of his eye, Smith flashed a glance at Lee squashed in the corner of the crowded compartment between the drunken sailor and the fat businessman reading *No Orchids for Miss Blandish*. In his cheap civilian clothes, complete with flat cap and white artificial silk scarf he looked completely out of place. Even the drunken sailor had looked strangely at him, as they had boarded the packed overnight train for Liverpool in London. 'Don't look like an effing lascar to me,' he had muttered before lapsing into a drunken sleep.

Now, as they started to run into a bombed-out Liverpool, Smith told himself he had to get rid of the American before they reached the ferry. With Lee, he didn't stand a chance of getting aboard and back to Eire with his precious secret. He screwed up his eyes and held his watch up to the thin blue light of the carriage's single bulb. Eight o'clock and the ferry sailed at midnight. He had four hours. But there was a catch. He knew the black man was armed. He had seen that bulge against his right inner leg and had guessed immediately what it was. The black American had a pistol strapped to his leg!

'Penny for 'em, mate?' the drunken sailor's cheery scouse voice broke into his thoughts.

He looked up startled. In the corner Lee stared at him hard. 'Penny for them...? Oh, yes, I was just wondering where a chap might get something to eat at this time of night in

Liverpool, just to put in time. I haven't got any coupons though,' Smith added.

'Fish and chips, if you're lucky,' the fat businessman reading *No Orchids* cut in. 'At this time of the night Liverpool is dead, since the bombings.'

'Except for the whores and the knocking shops,' the drunken sailor said cheerfully. 'Boom business these days. Ever since those Yankees started to sail in here, them liver birds have been more on their backs than on their feet.' He laughed at his own humour and the fat businessman frowned, closing his book. 'No need for that kind of talk, sailor,' he said severely. 'We all know the kind of life you sailors lead when you're on leave. Please spare us civilians from that kind of filth.'

The sailor grinned and held up his middle finger. 'Sit on that, mate!' he said.

The fat businessman flushed, opened his mouth to say something, then thought better of it. Instead he rose and fussed about with his case on the rack. The sailor winked drunkenly at Smith and took a half-smoked Woodbine from behind his ear. 'Give us a light for me coffin nail, mate, will yer?'

Smith obliged him and the sailor whispered a grateful 'ta', as he exhaled a stream of blue smoke directly into the other man's face. Suddenly Smith realized, as the train started to jerk to a stop and outside someone began to shout in a hard official voice, '*Draft for the Recce Regiment fall in over here...*,' that the drunken sailor could get them through the first hurdle; the Special Branch men and MPs who watched the barriers at every port railway station. Furtively he nodded to Lee. The black man nodded back and reached up for the brown paper parcel which now contained all his worldly goods. Involuntarily Smith's eyes were drawn to that bulge at his thigh. He told himself it would have to be sudden and quick. He couldn't allow the American to rip open his flies and get out the pistol.

Now everywhere the crowds of servicemen and shabby civilians were descending from the blacked-out train. The station was full of the usual hustle-and-bustle of wartime. Redcaps, tall and officious, striding the platforms in pairs on the lookout for deserters. Self-important RTO officers, with their red armbands and clipboards hurrying to and fro, collecting drafts. Prostitutes standing in the shadows, waiting for customers; and everywhere streams of pale-faced sailors returning to their ships, kitbags slung over their shoulders, artificial silk scarves knotted around their open necks, busily engaged in adjusting their caps before they hit the barriers and the waiting naval shore patrol.

Now the crowd from the London train began to funnel towards the barriers where the ticket collectors were poised with their clippers, the civilians to the left, the servicemen to the right, tickets, leave passes and travel documents at the ready.

Smith nudged Lee. Out of the corner of his mouth he hissed, 'Follow the sailor. He's pissed. They'll pick on him. Then off you go through, quick. Right?'

Lee nodded. 'Sure, get you.' He pushed himself behind the sailor, swaying somewhat now under the weight of his white kitbag and cursing under his breath. He too knew his problem. But once he was aboard that ferry, he knew he was safe. No one in Eire would care what his colour was. As for the ship to New York from Cobh, he would worry about New York and immigration when he got that far.

'Frigging hell!' the drunken sailor breathed in front of him, filling the air for a couple of square yards around with the stink of stale beer. 'Where's me bloody leave pass?' He stopped suddenly so that Lee nearly bumped into his back, and began fumbling inside his navy-blue raincoat with his free hand.

'Hey, you, sailor!' a harsh voice called. 'Keep moving. You're blocking the gangway.'

'Up yours!' the sailor answered, not looking up.

Opposite, the fat businessman in his bowler hat gasped and said, so that everyone could hear, 'What terrible language! I don't know what the country's coming to when people — even servicemen — can use that kind of language in public.' He tut-tutted furiously.

The sailor grinned and said loudly, 'Go on, Dad, stick yer thumb up yer ass and give yersen a cheap thrill!' He swayed badly and might well have fallen if it had not been for the big hand which now reached out and almost effortlessly dragged the sailor to the barrier. 'Leave-papers, sailor — and a bit smartish about it, too!'

The sailor did not even look up at the big red-faced petty officer who had grabbed hold of him. Instead, he dropped his kitbag and aimed a wild punch at him in one and the same movement. The petty officer yelped with pain. 'He's ferking well hit me,' he cried to no one in particular, bright-red blood jetting from his nose.

'*And I'll fuck well hit yer agen!*' the drunken sailor cried, carried away by it all now. He launched another punch at the bleeding petty officer, who stepped back hastily, bumped into the fat businessman who dropped his case, which flew open to reveal that it was filled with silken lace-frilled knickers.

'*Cor ferk a duck!*' one of the shore patrol breathed. 'Willyer look at them bleeding drawers! Puts a bloke on heat, just to look at them! Oh, my aching back!'

Smith didn't hesitate as the crimson-faced businessman bent down to try to stuff the frilly knickers back into the cheap suitcase. His right foot lashed out. The businessman yelled with pain. He went down among the knickers and in the same moment that the drunken sailor attempted to hit the bleeding petty officer for the third time, Smith pushed Lee and whispered urgently, '*Move!*'

The negro moved. He pushed his way through the milling, shouting crowd of excited civilians and soldiers, pushing his ticket into the hand of the startled collector, and was through and vanished into the outer darkness even before the MPs were aware he had done so. The first hurdle had been overcome, without difficulty…

''E's a good lad is our Jack,' the red-faced woman behind the counter was saying, as the dripping bubbled and spat in the big pan, wreathing her honest working class face in steam. 'Knocker-up in the morning then off to the docks at seven thirty and coming home after a twelve-hour shift to help me do the taties for the evening frying. He ain't a bad lad at all.' She emptied another bucket of chips into the bubbling fat and for a moment she vanished in steam.

Lee, standing next to Smith, stared at her and the shabby humble people in the queue around him as if they were creatures from another world. He had not understood one word the woman had said to the skinny blonde with no breasts in a flowered apron, who was standing by with the pile of squared newspaper, ready to wrap the first offerings from the steaming pan. *Jesus H. Christ!* He couldn't wait to get back to the land of the round doorknob and his own kind! He had had a bellyful of white folks, American and limey.

Smith, for his part, standing behind the negro in the crowded fish-and-chip shop, heavy with the smell of stale fat, human sweat, and working class defeat, stared at that bubbling, spitting brown fat as if mesmerized. He watched as the chips, pale and yellow an instant before, were already turning a deep crisp brown with that tremendous heat, the little bits of potatoes being thrust back and forth by its power, as if they had a life of their own. Put your hand in that pan by accident, he told himself, and it would be fried as crisp and brown as they were — *in seconds*!

He licked suddenly dried lips, but not in anticipation. Still he did not take his eyes off the bubbling fat.

The fat woman thrust a pan into the fat and brought out the first pile of steaming chips and emptied them into the warmer.

The skinny blonde with no breasts turned to the first in the queue, a toothless old man in the uniform of the Home Guard, wearing the fat ribbons of the Old War. 'What's yours, luv?' she asked, newspaper at the ready.

'One of each, luv,' he replied, 'with scraps please if you've got 'em?'

'No fish, luv,' she answered, busy shovelling chips into the paper.

'No fish!'

'No, luv. The lads at Fleetwood can't get out, ye see. Jerry subs, like.'

'Bloody Jerries! Been getting up my nose all my ruddy life,' the old Home Guard said indignantly. 'Plenty of scraps though.' He looked at Smith over his shoulder. 'D'yer hear that, no bleeding fish ... and I thought Churchill said we was winning the war.' He shook his grizzled old head. 'But I never did trust him, yer know. He had the troops shoot at workers back in the '26 strike, he did.'

Smith wasn't listening. His attention was fixed exclusively on the hot, spluttering brown fat, a sea of simmering, burning fury.

The old man sniffed and took up the tin salt-shaker. 'I suppose there's some salt left, eh Aggie? Churchill'll have left us a bit o' salt and vinegar at least, I don't doubt.'

Aggie, the fryer, laughed. 'Miserable old sod, aren't yer, Ebeneezer,' she said without rancour.

'Bleeding sauce!' the old man said and then hurried off with his parcel of chips clutched to his skinny chest, still muttering to himself about Churchill and the '26 Strike.

Now it was Lee's turn. Smith had briefed him on what to say. 'Bag o' chips, missus. No scraps.' And he said it quite well, though the blonde with no breasts looked at him strangely for a moment. Then she shrugged her skinny shoulders, as if dismissing him as one of the many strange seamen who flooded the port these days.

Smith jerked his head to the back of the shop, and said to the jolly woman frying, 'Can we eat 'em in here, missus? It's drizzling outside, like.'

'It's allus bleeding drizzling in Liverpool, luv,' she said a little wearily. She flashed a smile with her big yellow Panel teeth. 'Course ye can, luv!' She flung another bucket of chips into the pan. The fat hissed and spat angrily, wreathing her in steam once more.

'God,' Smith thought to himself. 'This place is one big firebomb!' He helped himself to salt and vinegar and edged to the back of the steam-filled shop. With his free hand, he felt the blacked-out door. The key was on the inside! Swiftly he palmed it, the plan beginning to form in his mind; while next to him, Lee pushed the chips into his mouth one by one in an absent-minded sort of a way, as if his thoughts were elsewhere…

CHAPTER 11

Dawn.

It was still cool. A slight breeze came from the pale green wash of the sea. Far out, the two hunted men could see a faint smudge of smoke. It might be the *Puerto de Barcelona* — the time and place were right — but Christian did not allow himself any false hopes, *yet!*

'They came this way all right, sir,' Frenssen said through cracked lips. He pointed to the scuffed sand and the small field-grey bag, the kind in which sailors carried their bread rations around with them. 'Somebody's dropped his nosebag.' He indicated the bag.

Christian, face haggard and unshaven, flashed a glance at the compass strapped to his wrist and nodded his agreement. 'Yes, as far as I can see *Kapitänleutnant* Gotha is steering a very accurate course. The question now is; is that the *Puerto* –'

The first shot, like the dry snap of a twig underfoot in a hot summer, cut into his words. The two of them spun round. About seven or eight hundred metres away, silhouetted a stark, sinister black against the first rays of the ascending sun, small figures had bridged the ridge, waving their arms, as if they were very angry — and to the right of the group, there were two of them mounted on camels!

Christian groaned.

Frenssen cursed. '*Shit!* Now the clock is frigging well really in the pisspot! They've found their frigging beasts of burden again.'

'Save yer breath,' Christian ordered grimly. 'Come on, let's see if we can double in this damned sand.' The two of them broke into a shambling trot. Behind them the Arabs cried angrily…

Now they could see the first stragglers of Thomas's party, struggling on wearily through the ankle-deep sand, carrying their machine pistols over their shoulders as farm labourers might bear their shovels after a hard day's toil in the fields.

Christian swallowed hard and tried to contain his hectic breathing. 'Hey, you lot, get moving! They're after us again… *Los, los, Männer!*'

The stragglers turned and saw their pursuers, the sudden fear all too obvious on their young faces. Abruptly they broke into an awkward run, all weariness forgotten now.

The cries of the Arabs grew louder. Christian swung round, Schmeisser in hand. The nearest Arabs, two of them mounted on camels, waving their long ancient rifles excitedly, were more than four hundred metres away, well out of range. But he knew he had to stop them somehow, even if it were only for a few moments. Every minute was precious. He clasped the machine pistol to his hip and loosed off a quick burst. The two Arabs tugged madly at the bits. The camels went down onto their haunches immediately. Swiftly the Arabs dropped off and took up a firing position, using the camels' ugly, moth-eaten bodies as protection.

Christian started to run again…

Now the whole column was in full flight. Panic was written on every face. They had come so far. No one wanted to die now. Already Thomas was standing up to his knees in the water, shirt stripped from his long skinny body, waving it frantically to the lone ship anchored out there, a lazy wisp of smoke drifting from its single funnel.

Suddenly Christian gasped and almost stopped running. A streak of grey had shot into the golden dawn sky. Next instant it exploded, an unreal, glowing, green colour. 'It's the signal,' he cried happily. 'Do you hear, you big rogue, that's the *Puerto de Barcelona!*'

'Ay,' Frenssen said grimly, throwing a glance over his shoulder, 'but do those buggers know it, sir... They're getting frigging close!'

'Come on ... keep running. If we can form a skirmish line —'

The lean grey camel came from nowhere. Abruptly it was cutting across their front, the Arab's rapacious, hook-nosed face set in a look of absolute triumph above the fringe of black beard.

Frenssen didn't even hesitate. As the Arab propped the long gun across the pommel of his saddle, he ripped off a swift burst. The slugs tore the length of the racing camel. Suddenly the grey hide was stitched a bloody red. The slugs raced towards the Arab. He threw up his hands, rifle dropping to the sand. He screamed and pitched out of the fringed saddle as the camel slid to its knees and slowly began to topple over on its side, the blood jetting in scarlet arcs from those terrible wounds. They ran on...

Thomas was here, there and everywhere, organizing the defence, as out to sea, the derricks lowered the first boat, and the Arabs pushed in their attack from both flanks. 'Come on, you bunch of cardboard soldiers!' he cried excitedly, as if he were enjoying the whole damned thing. 'Let's get your heads down. Here they come, and I'll have any man's arse who misses his target!'

Christian dived through the gap, followed an instant later by a gasping, crimson-faced Frenssen, and stared up at a transformed Trainburster Thomas. Even his dewdrop was missing from the end of his long nose.

Now the Arabs came racing in, on camelback and on foot, screaming shrilly, waving their firearms, here and there a curved sword gleaming silver in the rays of the ascending sun. A ragged volley broke out the length of the German line. Here and there an Arab went down, arms flailing the air as if the wounded man was climbing the rungs of an invisible ladder. But still the rest came on, confident of victory, knowing the white men had nowhere to retreat to — save the sea.

Christian controlled his crazy breathing with difficulty. With hands that trembled like leaves, his vision blurred and uncertain, he raised his Schmeisser. To his immediate front two Arabs were racing forward through the sand, weapons raised, dark, hawklike faces set in looks of triumph. He pressed the trigger. The machine pistol slammed into his shoulder. He gasped, blinked, and groaned. His aim had been so unsteady that he had missed them by metres!

The Arabs shouted something and increased their pace. One of them had slung his rifle and had drawn a long, wicked-looking knife.

'Christ on a crutch!' Frenssen, squatting next to Christian, cursed fearfully, 'Let that fucker get near yer and yer've lost yer outside plumbing in zero, comma, nothing seconds!'

He ripped up his machine pistol and fired. The Arab stopped as if he had just run into an invisible wall. Bewildered, he stared down at his intestines which were beginning to slip out of his savaged stomach like a grey-green, steaming serpent. Next moment he went down onto his knees, wailing and weeping as he tried to stuff them back into the gaping red hole which had suddenly appeared in his stomach.

But the other one was not to be stopped. Suddenly he was leaping across the little sand parapet. He lashed out with his rifle. Frenssen yelled and went reeling back, a great gory weal rising up along the side of his cropped head. In an instant Christian felt himself smothered as the Arab slammed into him. His nostrils were assailed by the cloying, rancid smell of a long unwashed body. Skinny hands sought and found his upturned throat.

The pressure was tremendous. Silver stars started to explode in front of his eyes. Desperately he writhed back and forth, but still he could not shake off the Arab, who stared down at him, his cruel lean face, with its great hooked nose, set and determined. Now he was going. Christian could feel it. His lungs threatened to explode. He must have air ...*he must*!

His ears started popping. Frantically he brought up his knee. The Arab laughed and avoided it easily. Now all was a great roaring redness. He was going ... he was going... In a moment he would be dead... Suddenly it didn't matter anymore — nothing mattered... It might as well be now as later. Tamely, as all resistance fled from his emaciated, exhausted body, he submitted, letting it happen to him.

But *Kapitänleutnant* Christian Jungblut was not fated to die in this remote place. Dimly he heard the crack, the shrill scream and then the pressure had gone and the breath came flooding back into his lungs so that suddenly he was gasping and choking like a condemned man abruptly cut down from the gallows.

Weakly he opened his eyes and blinked them several times. Thomas came into focus, wavering and trembling as if seen through a heat haze. In his hands he held an upturned Schmeisser, the steel butt flushed a dark gory red, flecked with gleaming white pieces which might have been ivory, but which

Christian knew instinctively were bone. To his side lay the Arab, dead, the back of his skinny skull smashed in. 'Do you think that qualifies me for the combat infantryman's badge, Christian?' he heard Thomas ask from a long way away, a grin of triumph on his skinny stupid face.

Christian couldn't even curse…

Now the two boats were a kilometre away, their crews seemingly unaware of the tragedy in the making on the beach; they took their time, rowing leisurely, as if they were savouring the early morning exercise.

Christian, his throat swollen and as rough as sand-paper, cursed. 'The shits must be blind, Thomas!' he said thickly. 'Can't they see the Arabs? Can't they hear the firing?'

'Spaniards,' Thomas said calmly and, whipping up his machine pistol, fired a controlled burst at a group of Arabs crawling ever closer to the left flank of the little perimeter. '*Komm' ich heute nicht, komm' ich morgen,* you know their sort. *Mañana*, they call it.'

'*Fuck Mañana!*' Christian said crudely. 'There'll be no *mañana* for us if they don't get here soon. We're running out of ammo — and look, another bunch of the swine has arrived.' He indicated the height, where now a group of camel-riders had positioned themselves and were surveying the scene below. 'They're coming from all over Africa for the loot,' he added miserably.

'Not to worry,' Thomas said calmly. 'We'll take care of them all right, Christian.'

For a moment Christian stared at the other officer almost in wonder. Old unlucky Trainburster Thomas had been transformed by combat. That customary miserable hangdog look of his had vanished. Even here, with their lives at stake, he seemed confident and happy. Ten years had been wiped off his face. In spite of the imminent disaster, as the Arabs massed for yet another charge on the little beach perimeter, Christian said hoarsely, 'You're enjoying this, aren't you, Thomas?'

The other officer beamed at him happily. 'Yes, quite frankly, now you ask, Christian, I am. I've never felt so great, so full of life ever before. I think it must be the adrenalin hitting the old blood stream… Now listen, Christian,' he added urgently as up on the ridge the Arabs started to chant their battle cries, working themselves up for the assault, 'this is what we're going to do. I know it's risky,' he held up his hand, as if Christian might well protest, 'but it's the only way. You're going to take half the men, when I give the signal, and swim for it.'

'And you?' Christian heard himself rasp tamely, as if it were every day that a greenhorn like Thomas gave orders to a veteran like himself who had been decorated three times for bravery in action by the Führer himself.

'I'm going to cover the retreat,' he answered happily, 'thinning out my line gradually. By dividing the force in half, the rest of us will have more ammo.'

'And the last ones? The Arabs will rush the perimeter, you know, once they see us in the water.'

'Oh, the devil will take the hindmost, Christian,' Thomas replied lightly. 'I'm a fine swimmer. I was almost picked for the '36 Olympics, you know.'

'They weren't shooting at the competitors back then, remember,' Christian said sourly.

Thomas did not seem to hear. 'All right, start pulling every second man back to the water's edge and get ready. Here the buggers come again!'

Christian flung a look up the slope. The Arabs were charging all-out. He had never realized that camels could run that fast.

Dust and sand spurting up at their flying hooves, their long ugly necks stuck out, hair trailing, they raced towards the perimeter, their riders waving their weapons and shrieking, carried away by the wild, unreasoning blood-lust of the desert.

Suddenly he was attacked by a crazy fear. He didn't want to be left behind to die in this arsehole of the world. *He wanted to live*! Abruptly he was crawling from hole to hole, repeating Thomas's orders, while Frenssen, big feet spread apart like a western gunslinger in some movie shoot-out, stood fearlessly in the semi-circle of the defence, loosing off controlled bursts to left and right.

Men and steeds went down everywhere. Here and there, their riders dead in the saddle, the crazed camels kept on running only to be mown down in the last instant by that merciless fire. Suddenly the steam went out of the Arab attack. One of them, perhaps a sheik, stood high in his stirrups and cried an order.

As one the survivors turned and fled, but not far. Everywhere they began dropping effortlessly from their high perches into the sand, while the camels continued their wild flight, and started sniping the defenders below. Now the German line was only separated from them by a hundred metres of open ground. Christian, still carried away by that unreasoning fear, knew it was time to go. They hadn't many minutes left. 'Drop your weapons!' he cried, 'give them to the man nearest to you… Off with your shoes and upper clothing… Come on now —'

'But sir!' Frenssen protested angrily, busily engaged in fitting another magazine into his machine pistol.

'*Not a word*!' Christian cut him short harshly. '*Obermaat*, hand over your weapon and get the hell outa here!'

In disgust Frenssen flung his machine pistol down next to the sweating young sailor, blood dripping from a red crease across his forehead. 'Keep yer shitting turnip down, sailor,' he said. 'Them's not frigging fried sausages they're firing!'

'*Danke, Obermaat,*' the young sailor gasped. He dropped the pistol he had been using up to now and grabbed the machine pistol, a look of absolute happiness on his face, as if he had just been given some tremendous Christmas present.

'Wet behind the spoons,' Frenssen grumbled and dug his hands in his pockets stubbornly. 'Lot of frigging wet-tails!' Deliberately, contemptuously, he began to stroll to the edge of the water where the others were already beginning to wade out, face set in a scowl.

Christian ignored him. '*Obermaat*, bring up the rear. I hope all these men can swim, but you never know these days.' He shaded his eyes against the slanting rays of the new sun. The two boats were about four hundred metres away now, the crews resting passively on their oars, watching the proceedings on shore in an almost bored manner like a scratch crew might observe some crack rowing team at a peacetime regatta.

Christian cursed. The spaghetti-eaters were not going to risk their necks this day. 'All right, off you go the rest of you. Swim, will you. *Frigging well start swimming. At the double now!*'

Now the Arabs were pushing home their attack. They rose, fired, doubled a few paces, taking casualties all the time, but advancing steadily. They knew victory was theirs. They could see the white men already pushing waist-deep into the water, obviously heading for the waiting boat and they guessed that the perimeter must have been thinned out.

Standing up to his ankles in water, watching Frenssen plunge after the rest of the 'wet-tails', as he called them scornfully, Christian saw the first splashes as long shots began to hit the water. It wouldn't be long now before the Arabs rushed them. He spun round and, cupping his hands above the snap-and-crackle of small-arms fire, shouted, 'Thomas, for God's sake, start pulling them back now, man!'

Trainburster Thomas, face red and glistening with sweat, looked hastily over his shoulder and yelled happily, 'Five more minutes, Christian! I can hold them another five minutes… Going to thin out my line, every second man again, in half a mo… Will you take charge?'

'But Thomas…' The words dried on his lips. Thomas was no longer listening. He was on his feet again, damned left hand folded behind his back as if he were going on some stupid peacetime range, snapping off well-aimed shots to left and right. Christian groaned. Five years of nothing but failure and now Trainburster Thomas thought he'd cure his desire for a medal out here in the middle of nowhere, fighting off a lot of brigands. What a hope.

A camel-rider sprang over the sand wall, dropped easily like an athlete to the ground, grabbed one of the machine pistols which the first group had left behind and pelted towards the men in the water, the gun already chattering at his side.

Bullets zipped towards the swimming men. Little angry gusts of white water erupted everywhere. A man yelled, his scream ending in a sudden gurgle, as his hands went straight upwards, the water suddenly turning pink, and he disappeared without another sound.

Christian dived at the Arab. They went down in a wildly flailing bundle of arms and legs. Christian slammed his hand, palm upwards, against the base of the Arab's nose. There was a click. He lay still, his neck broken. Now Christian could wait no longer. 'Thomas,' he yelled fervently, angrily, 'fall back … fall back, while you've still got a chance, you silly bastard!'

Thomas waved his Schmeisser in acknowledgement. 'All right, you men,' he cried happily, 'into the water... I'll cover the rear. Off you go — *into the water*!'

Now as the remaining men at the perimeter broke and started streaming back towards the water, and the Arabs put in their final attack, Thomas threw all caution to the wind. Standing upright in the middle of the perimeter, a spare Schmeisser slung over his skinny shoulders, he fired quick controlled bursts, making the Arabs pay in blood for every metre of ground they gained, falling back stubbornly under the pressure, fighting all the time.

Christian groaned suddenly. Thomas was down on one knee. He could see the abrupt patch of bright scarlet on the faded cloth. But a moment later he was up again, fitting a new magazine into his machine pistol, and firing almost instantly.

Now he could wait no longer. The last of the men were splashing frantically into the water or flinging themselves forward in fast shallow dives. '*Thomas*!' he yelled desperately.

Thomas swung round, his face happy and lathered in sweat. 'Remember the combat infantryman's badge, Christ —'

The bullet struck him squarely in the chest. A horrified Christian could see the little red puff at the back of his shirt as it cut right through him and came out at the other side. Thomas's face seemed to crumble. His knees began to give. The Schmeisser tumbled from nerveless fingers to the sand.

For one long moment he knelt there on the ground like a boxer refusing to go down for a count of ten. Suddenly, startlingly, he flopped forward — *dead*!

The Arabs were charging forward now, yelling with triumph, stopping only to pick up the precious weapons abandoned by the sailors. Christian flung himself into the water in a tremendous racing dive and broke into the fastest crawl he knew, churning up the still water at a terrific rate as he headed for the boats, praying that the Arabs wouldn't wade in further than their skinny knees. Behind him, sprawled out on the beach, sightless eyes staring unseeingly at that perfect blue morning sky, *Kapitänleutnant* Thomas Gotha lay dead. Trainburster Thomas had won — and lost — his only battle, *on land…*

CHAPTER 12

'*There's a bluebird over the white cliffs of Dover*,' the muffled singing penetrated the still fish-and-chip shop now from the little pub opposite.

The red-faced frying woman looked at her watch. 'Won't be long now,' she said to the girl with no breasts. 'Mr Ramsbotham'll turn 'em out at ten... He told me this morning, he won't last the week with his beer ration from the brewery.'

'Ay,' the blonde said and picked up her bundle of cut newspaper in readiness.

At the range, the red-faced woman opened the pan to reveal the bubbling brown fat and raised a bucket of chips to throw them in. Smith knew he could wait no longer. He crumpled the greasy paper and stepped forward from the back of the blacked-out fish shop, as if he was wondering what to do with the paper.

Lee, toying with the french fries, as Smith had told him to do so as to spin out time till the ferry left, watched him carefully. He didn't trust Smith. Now the limey, or whatever he was, knew the great secret and could double-cross him. He had to keep his eyes on him all the time. Not that he was scared by the other man, with his bent, skinny shoulders and weak fingers. Besides, the limey was unarmed — he'd already checked that — and he had the fat cook's .45. He touched it softly through the coarse serge of his cheap suit and felt reassured.

'Give it me, luv,' the blonde with no breasts said pleasantly enough, 'I'll get rid of it —'

In the same instant that she reached out to take the crumpled ball of newspaper from Smith, he acted with startling suddenness. He grabbed the pile of newspaper and flung it with a grunt at the open pan of fat. It splashed everywhere, bursting into flame immediately as it struck the red-hot exterior of the old cast-iron range. The fryer reeled back screaming, the burning fat running up her pail and along her brawny arm, the flesh beginning to bubble and blister obscenely at once. The blonde with no breasts screamed. She ran forward to aid her friend. Instantly her floral apron was aflame too. She tore at it hysterically with hands that began to melt immediately.

Lee started from his corner. '*What the hell —*'

Smith kicked him neatly in the stomach and he went sprawling backwards, missed his steps on the greasy floor tiles and sat down abruptly. Smith didn't give him a chance to recover. He bolted for the door. With fingers that trembled wildly, he sought to thrust the key in the lock.

Across the road in the blacked-out pub they were chanting, '*Now this is number one and he's got her on the run, roll me over, lay me down and do it agen!*' with the landlord bellowing and ringing his bell. '*Time, gentlemen. TIME, GENTLEMEN, PLEASE!*'

They wouldn't hear, Smith told himself, as he thrust home the key and turned it swiftly. From inside now there came the muffled screams of the dying women and the smell of frying, though this time it wasn't chips. Lee thudded his shoulder against the door, but it was stout and Victorian, just like the shop itself. He wouldn't be able to break it down in a hurry.

Holding on for all he was worth, a frantic Smith shot a glance at the shop's window. It was well blacked-out with a wooden-screen. Even if Lee had strength enough to heave something through the glass on the other side, it wouldn't make any difference.

'Let me out, for Chrissake, *let me out!*' He could hear Lee's tortured voice, muffled by the thick oak door, above the screams of the women. The heat was becoming more intense by the second. He could feel it already. Near where the burning range was, the outer bricks were beginning to glow a faint pink. The window went. He could hear the crackling of the glass as it splintered, melted and tumbled down. Desperately he held on.

Behind him the wartime street was deserted. There weren't even the usual lovers lurking in the air raid shelter at the corner under the little blue light. In the pub they were bellowing, *'Now this is number two and he's got it up her flue…'*

Smith, hands tightened in a vice-like grip on the doorhandle, felt himself begin to sweat. The heat was terrific. Already the paint on the outside of the door was beginning to bubble and burst like the symptoms of some loathsome skin disease. His nostrils were assailed by its stink and the sweeter smell of burning flesh. From within, the screams were getting fainter. It would be over soon. Fat, slippy and steaming, was beginning to drip out under the door…

'For God's sake, Smith!' Lee wailed piteously from within and he could feel the knob being twisted. He held on madly, the veins bulging at his temples, his eyes wild and wide like those of a crazy man.

'Smith!'

Suddenly there was the sound of firing. Near his knees the wood splintered and he felt a hot pain in his side, as if someone had just thrust a heated poker into his soft flesh. Smith screamed shrilly and fell back from the door, the blood already streaming down his thigh.

Now there was the sound of hacking and tearing at the wood. One last shot and suddenly the burning door was swinging inwards to reveal the thing standing swaying there, beyond the two bodies merrily burning, a charred black already on the tiled floor, one hand extended like a burned branch.

In spite of his wound, Smith gasped and fell back a few paces more. Instead of a face there was only a black crusted mask which bubbled here and there a loathsome pink. Where the eyes should have been, there were two vivid scarlet pits. With agonizing slowness the thing raised that one charred hand, the bones gleaming through the blackness a startling ivory-white.

'No!' Smith croaked, raising one arm in front of his face, as if to blot out this terrible thing, which had started to totter towards him blindly, feeling its way with that terrible charred claw. He slumped against a lamp-post, petrified by this monstrous thing advancing upon him, strange inhuman, animal sounds coming from the red hole of the mouth which could have signified anything.

It stumbled. Smith thought it was down. But no! It righted itself in a hideous stiff manner, glowing a blood-red against the flames of the fish shop now, that one obscene limb stretched out in front of it.

'No, *please*, NO!' Smith screamed as those charred white fingers touched his face, contorted, blanched with absolute, unreasoning fear. 'I didn't —'

The hole which was once a mouth opened. Meaningless sounds emerged from it as the red strips of flesh hanging from the legs still smouldered sickeningly.

Smith cowered back, trying to avoid that terrible claw. '*No* … *no, no*—'

The gas cylinders which heated the dripping exploded suddenly. Smith felt himself dragged from his feet, as if by some giant invisible hand, and flung right across the street. He gasped with shock as his body struck the icy water of the fire brigade's static water tank. He went under, spitting and spluttering, in the same moment that the fish shop went up in one great all-consuming burst of flame, leaving behind nothing but a loud-echoing silence, broken only by the sudden cries of alarm from the pub, and that terrible charred thing lying on the blazing pavement like a calcinated log...

BOOK TWO: CONVOY TO CATASTROPHE

'The thought just occurred
That we're nobody's children
At all, after all.'
David Bowie; 'After All'

CHAPTER 1

'The Twenty-Second Infantry, sir, the Fourth Division!' the bespectacled driver, who had complained all the way from Plymouth about 'my goddam draft board,' announced with surprising formality, and stopped the big olive drab Packard at the gate just opposite the big Stars and Stripes and the smaller flag of the 22nd.

Savage, sitting bolt upright in the back, his lean face bronzed, hard and very tough, frowned. Security wasn't particularly tight in this particular sector of the European Theatre of Operations, he told himself, when goddam drivers acted like tourist guides.

A lone PFC with his rifle slung over his shoulder, moodily chewing gum, appeared from somewhere, helmet cocked to one side like John Wayne in *Bataan*, He recognized the leaf on Savage's collar and gave a half-hearted salute. Savage returned it sharply, energetically, as if he were back at the Point.

Savage wheeled down the window and felt the cold damp Devon air creep in. 'I'm to report to Colonel Lanham,' he snapped.

'Sure, sir, okay sir,' the sentry said easily. 'Drive two blocks down the company street and you'll see RHQ right in front of you. Big sign on it. Can't miss it, Colonel, sir.'

'Thank you, soldier,' Savage answered crisply, noting automatically that the PFC hadn't asked for his papers. He rolled up the window again as the driver shivered and thrust home first gear. They began to move again between wooden huts and tents, their canvas flapping in the stiff breeze which came from the cold grey sea beyond the cliff.

Savage didn't seem to be looking, but in reality his eyes were everywhere, noting the sloppiness of the huts and the slow, careless way in which the GIs saluted, those who did salute him. Behind one of the huts, he caught a quick glimpse of two fat sergeants shooting craps in the cropped grass. He flashed a glance at his watch. It was inscribed, a present from his battalion when he had left the Third. It was just ten after eight. He concluded that the 22nd Infantry was not exactly over-disciplined. He smiled darkly to himself and stroked the bayonet scar that ran the length of the right side of his face, another 'souvenir' of Italy last year. Finally the car stopped. He sprang out energetically, folder clasped in his gloved hands. He paused in front of the long mirror beside the wooden steps, bearing the legend, '*Are you a credit to your outfit?*' He tugged his short greatcoat tighter and adjusted his overseas cap. He liked what he saw.

He thrust open the swing-door without knocking; why should he? Two fat, pasty-faced clerks slumped behind their typewriters while another sat on the desk, mug of coffee in hand, saying, 'So I sez to her, if it wasn't for them goddam barrage balloons of yourn, your whole goddam island would sink —'

The words froze on his lips as he saw the tall, trim officer with the hard grey eyes standing there framed in the doorway, his insignia burnished and gleaming as if he had just come from recruit training. He sprang to his feet, crying, 'Welcome to the Twenty-Second, Colonel, sir!' He faked a warm smile. 'Glad to have you aboard, sir.' He gave Savage a sloppy salute.

Savage returned it precisely, crisply. 'Thank you,' he barked, again not liking what he saw. 'I have an appointment with Colonel Lanham.'

'Yessir ... immediately, sir,' the fat clerk bowed from the waist, one hand extended like a *maître de* in some fancy restaurant inviting an honoured guest to step closer. Savage frowned. But he said nothing. As a new boy, it was wiser to keep one's mouth shut, for a while at least.

The clerk crossed the office and knocked at the door opposite while the other two made a great show of hammering away at their typewriters. Savage wasn't impressed.

'Colonel Savage ... how good to see you!' A small nut-brown officer stood there, wearing a plain heavy wool OD shirt and trousers and no badges of rank, beaming at him.

Savage snapped to attention and saluted smartly.

The little colonel, who was Lanham, returned the salute equally smartly and Savage saw the West Point class ring on his hand. Lanham was a professional like himself.

'Buck,' he said, extending his hand, 'call me Buck, Savage.'

'Sam... Sam Savage, sir, er Buck,' the younger officer replied shaking the hand. It was firm, dry and hard, unlike so many of the hands he had shaken ever since he had arrived in England. The planners were living high on the hog in London, he had realized, getting fat and slow. Too many dames, dinners and classy booze.

'Come on into the office. Let's shoot the breeze for a while, Sam.' The little colonel shot a hard glance at the three fat clerks. 'And for God's sake, you three goof-offs, willya get some goddam work done instead of polishing your goddam nails all the time!'

The biggest of the three giggled like a woman. Lanham frowned and kicked back the door behind Savage — *hard!*

'All right,' he barked as soon as Savage had seated himself and lit his favourite old corn-cob pipe, 'I won't bullshit you,

Sam. The Twenty-Second, indeed the whole goddam Fourth Division, is one hell of a mess!'

Savage said nothing. Through the dirty window of the hut he could see a group of KP men shuffling by with their mops over their shoulders, pails in hand, as if they were a southern chain-gang.

'For an outfit which is going to spearhead the attack of the US Army into Europe before this summer is out, Sam, we're hopeless. The Krauts will make mincemeat of us. That's why *I'm* here,' he poked a finger at his skinny chest and looked hard at the tall, immaculate veteran through the old-fashioned granny spectacles he affected, '*and you*! We're gonna have to make them get the lead outa their butts — but *quick*!'

'Yes, Buck,' Savage said dutifully, as always playing it with his cards close to his chest. Ever since he had left the Point, he had found that to be the best policy.

'Now you, Sam, have had a fine combat record with the Third in North Africa, Sicily and Italy — I've read your record. Three assault landings, two purple hearts, the Silver Star and the DSC. Not bad for a guy who's just pushing thirty, not bad at all.' He beamed. 'You're exactly the kind of officer we urgently need in a Division which has sat on its duff here in the UK since 1942. You know what the dough-faces say; "*The Fourth'll be here cleaning the bluebird shit off the white cliffs of Dover till the end of the century*!" ' He laughed and Savage chuckled with him, but his cold blue eyes did not light up. Sam Savage hadn't smiled for a long time now; he had had no cause to.

The little regimental colonel rose from behind his desk and strode over to the map of France pinned on the wall. It was not a military map, just one of the kind that might well have been cut from some newspaper or magazine, cheap and not very well detailed. 'Come on over here, Sam,' he commanded, 'and get a load of this.'

Savage did so and frowned.

The colonel chuckled. 'Just security, Sam, just security. Nobody's gonna learn anything from that map, and brother, security is surely horseshit in this camp.' He lowered his voice, face suddenly very serious. 'All right, Sam, I'm gonna let you into the big secret. One word outside this office of what I'm gonna tell you now and you're canned. Only last week, Ike had to send a two-star general — commander of the Ninth Air Force — back home because he shot off his mouth at Claridge's. So, keep this firmly under your hat.'

Savage tensed and felt suddenly excited. The little colonel was no feather merchant or canteen commando after all, like most of them he had encountered since he had arrived here. Perhaps the Fourth wasn't going to be such a shit deal after all. He nodded swiftly and said, 'You can rely on me, sir — er, Buck.'

The colonel squinted through his old-fashioned glasses at the cheap map and pointed. 'Normandy. That's where we're going to land.'

Savage gasped, taken by surprise. He had just been told one of the greatest secrets of the war; where the Allies were going to attack *Festung Europa*.

'The US Army will put up two and a bit assault divisions. The Big Red One,' he grinned wryly at the nickname, 'will attack here, together with a regiment of the Twenty-Ninth Division, at Vierville and St Laurent, code-named Omaha.' He let his words sink in. 'We of the Fourth will land — here — just in front of the hamlet of St Martin on the other side of the River Vire. Our objective is code-named *Utah*!' He looked directly at Savage over the top of his gold-rimmed glasses, and said very solemnly, 'Now, Sam, you know one of the greatest secrets of this war.' He paused. 'And why am I telling you it, something that a lot of top brass in London don't know?' He answered his own question. 'Because I want you to lead my First Battalion, the one which will hit the beaches first. You've done it three times before, Sam. I'm asking you to do it one more time. And Sam, make a success of it, too. A lot, a real lot, perhaps the future of the West depends upon it.' The words were said without pathos, but Colonel Savage could feel the pent-up emotion behind them.

'I'll do my best, Buck,' he said simply.

'That's my boy!' Colonel Lanham beamed at him. 'So now you know the great secret. You have become what top brass has code-named *a Bigot*.'

Savage savoured the new word and grinned wryly. 'Funny name, Buck. "Torch," "Husky," and now, "Bigot". Where in Sam Hill does the Pentagon get them from?'

The little colonel was not listening, it seemed. Instead he was staring out of the window, watching the pale young faces of his men as they passed.

Savage looked at him, wondering what he was thinking as he looked at the soldiers whose destiny lay in his hands. Was he wondering whether they could do it on the day — storm those beaches and take the German positions? Was he considering how many of them would be dead — dead before they had begun to live — before this year was out?

Savage shook his head. He had long realized that a man who commanded men in battle, sent them to their deaths, should not think a lot, at least about that. If you did, you went crazy in the end, or simply stopped functioning effectively. Then the head-shrinkers called it 'combat fatigue' and quietly shipped you off back to the States.

Softly Savage cleared his throat.

The little colonel started and woke from his reverie. 'Sorry, Sam, just day-dreaming. Now,' he was crisp and businesslike again, 'there's only one other thing, now that you are a Bigot.'

'Yes, Buck?'

'On no account must you fall into enemy hands before the Invasion. They tell me that the Germans have ways of even making a mummy talk.' He laughed, but there was no warmth in it.

'I doubt if I'll be falling into enemy hands here in Devon, Buck,' Savage said.

The other man didn't seem to hear. Instead he said, 'Ike has ordered that the strictest security must be enforced with every single Bigot. Every time you're down there at Slapton Sands, coming in from the bay on exercise, you've got to be escorted, Sam. Ike ordered the divisional commander, General Barton, to ensure that it was put into immediate effect. I'm under escort myself when I'm down there.'

'I see,' Savage said, though in fact he didn't.

The little colonel strode briskly to the door, flung it open and cried, 'Jenkins, stop doing your frigging nails again and send in Hunt.'

Jenkins giggled and said, 'Yessir.'

The little colonel left the door open and waited there, while Savage stared at him, wondering what was coming next. He didn't have to wait long. A minute or so later, the colonel was ushering a slight, somewhat embarrassed young soldier into the office, kicking the door shut behind him with the heel of his boot, while Savage stared at the man.

'Private First Class Hunt — "*Peewee*" Hunt naturally on account of his size. Even I'm big in comparison.' The small soldier with the youthful freckled face blushed and then blushed even more when the colonel said, 'And the best shot in the whole Regiment, aren't you, Peewee?'

'So they say, sir,' the soldier answered in a slow Texan drawl.

'Now, Peewee, I have assigned you to be Colonel Savage's personal escort during training and you are to be armed at all times. Probably a Colt forty-five would be the best weapon. Get the quartermaster to sign you out one as soon as you leave here.'

'Yessir.'

Savage frowned. He didn't like the idea of an escort. He had known back in the line in Italy some nervous nellies with bodyguards who went round with them at the front, armed like walking arsenals. He'd always thought such bodyguards made a bad impression on the dough-faces. There were no bodyguards for them when they were in combat, why should their commanders be specially protected?

The little colonel saw the look on Savage's taut bronzed face and said hastily, 'No, Sam, Peewee here isn't there to protect you. No sir!' He looked from the colonel to the little soldier and then back again swiftly. 'No, if there is any possibility that you might fall into German hands, Sam, Peewee is going to do one thing.'

'And what's that, sir?' the soldier asked curiously.

The colonel hesitated only an instant before snapping harshly, '*You are to shoot Colonel Savage dead!*'

CHAPTER 2

The little patrol boat rocked and swayed in the middle of the Bay of Danzig, while the assembled U-boat skippers waited for the somewhat pompous officer from the experimental torpedo school to begin his address.

Christian looked around at his fellow skippers. Most of their chests were devoid of the 'good' pieces of 'tin'. All of them wore the combat submariner's badge, of course, but otherwise their decorations were limited to the Iron Cross, Second Class, with here and there the gilt blaze of the 'Order of the Scrambled Egg', as the old hares called the 'German Cross in Gold' cynically. Indeed he'd noticed the others eyeing his own Knight's Cross, complete with Laurel Leaves, enviously. Obviously at twenty-seven he was a very old hare to them, an 'ace' to be treated with due deference. Suddenly Christian Jungblut felt old, and not a little jaded, too.

The torpedo expert who affected an old-fashioned starched winged collar which marked him as a pre-war big ship man, cleared his throat noisily and barked, '*Meine Herren*, may I have your attention, please?'

Christian grinned suddenly. How the fat pompous officer, who was at least forty and still a lieutenant with no decorations, must hate lecturing to these brash, confident young submariners half his age! In the *Kriegsmarine*, the big ships were out, most of them tucked up impotently in Norwegian and French harbours. This was the year of the U-boat. Poor bastard, he'd retire a lieutenant! Still, Christian told himself, suddenly sombre, most of the young lieutenant-commanders he was soon going to lecture would never reach the age of thirty. They'd be long dead, including probably himself, by the time final victory was achieved, if it ever was.

'What you are going to see, gentlemen,' he commenced, as the light finally went and the Bay of Danzig was suddenly an inky black, 'is the performance of two new torpedoes which will revolutionize U-boat warfare. First, we will show you what we call the — er — *destroyer killer*, the T-5 torpedo. After that, my chaps will demonstrate the brand new — and I must warn you urgently against any careless talk, gentlemen — the LUT. Both are top-secret and potential war-winners.' He cleared his throat pompously again and let his words sink in.

But if he expected his listeners, grouped there in faint blue aft, to be impressed, he was doomed to disappointment. They all feigned boredom, as if they had seen it all before — and then some. One said languidly, 'I say, speed it up, will you. It's cold out here and I've really got a very delicate chest!' A more robust voice called, '*Himmel, Arsch und Wolkenbruch*, step on it, I've got a very hot body waiting for me in Danzig. Even if she is a Polack, I'm not racially prejudiced — as long as she's got *it* in the right spot!'

There was muted laughter and the ex-big ship man decided he couldn't impress this cheeky rabble, so he 'stepped on it'. 'Both torpedoes are battery driven so there will be no tell-tale wake, as with the other models, and for this demonstration they will be equipped with luminous, dummy warheads so that you will be able to follow their course without difficulty.' He called out an order and on the blacked-out bridge the telegraph sounded. The little patrol boat surged forward. Suddenly the ribald chatter and laughter died away. All of these young men who would soon be sailing to do battle with the Anglo-Americans knew just how much their lives depended on new weapons and techniques.

'Here's the first one!' the big ship officer called sharply. 'To port!'

Christian's eyes narrowed as he tried to penetrate the gloom. Next to him the young skipper cried excitedly. 'There … *there's the tin fish!*'

Christian spotted the green iridescent light in the dark water. It was heading straight for the little patrol boat. He saw, too, there was none of the usual tell-tale wake which had betrayed the presence of a U-boat so often in the past.

Up on the bridge, the skipper of the patrol boat flung his craft hastily to starboard. The U-boat captains grabbed for support as the vessel's superstructure almost touched the water. The new torpedo changed course immediately.

Now the patrol boat skipper threw his little ship into a series of wild manoeuvres, zig-zagging violently almost as if a drunken man had taken over the bridge. But still the homing torpedo clung to the craft persistently, doggedly reducing the distance between itself and the ship.

'My God!' the young skipper next to Christian whispered in awe, as the torpedo disappeared beneath the patrol ship's stern to reappear, execute an elegant loop, and come zooming in once more, 'it's frigging well almost human… It can think for itself just like a human being!'

'*Better!*' the demonstration officer snapped, obviously very pleased with himself, as if he had invented the new weapon personally. 'Unlike a human being, it doesn't get flustered, have nerves, or make the wrong move when under pressure.'

Christian, too, was impressed, as finally the torpedo's batteries gave out and it surfaced like some monstrous dead fish, its bright headlight glowing in the water. Yet he heard himself saying loudly, above the excited chatter of the others, 'A stunning performance, *Herr Oberleutnant*, but what good is a brand new tin fish like that to us, if we can't get within striking distance thanks to the Tommies' damned air-to-ground radar and all the other devilish tricks they've got tucked up their sleeves?'

There was a murmur of agreement from the others.

The demonstration officer peered at Christian in the thin blue light and said, 'Oh, it's the ace, *Kapitänleutnant* Jungblut, isn't it?'

There was no mistaking that malicious note in the way 'ace' was pronounced and Christian clenched his fists in sudden anger. All these 'rear echelon stallions' were the same. They took every available opportunity they could find of taking a rise out of the 'front swine'. He supposed it was due to envy and the knowledge, that comforting knowledge, that they weren't going to have to take their precious bones to market; they'd survive.

'Yes,' he snapped, 'and show some damned respect when you're speaking to a superior officer, *Herr Oberleutnant!*'

'Please excuse me, *Herr Kapitänleutnant,*' the other man said hastily, then added quickly, 'The other model, the new LUT torpedo, is created to solve the problem you had in mind, sir. It is designed to overcome your inability to launch a torpedo at close range due to Allied defensive measures. It can be released at a great distance from a convoy and directed to pursue the enemy ships along its mean track, describing any number of predetermined loops, of any selected size, and at any chosen depth. A handful of LUTs released in a screening pattern could form an effective barrier ahead of an enemy convoy without the attacking submarine having to penetrate the convoy's defences.'

'*Bullshit*!' Christian answered coldly. He had taken an instinctive dislike to the older man and made no attempt to hide it. 'You're trying to blind us with bullshit, *Oberleutnant*!'

There was a chuckle from some of the young skippers and others said indignantly, 'Yes, it's our lives which are at stake!'

'You still haven't answered my question. Wonder weapons, I shit on them from a great height!' Christian persisted bitterly. 'What good are they if we haven't got the right vehicle to launch them, eh?'

The older man sighed like some resigned grammar school teacher confronted by the class's loud-mouth yet once again.

'All in good time, *Herr Kapitänleutnant*, all in good time. You are forgetting the Century class boats, aren't you…?'

Christian started visibly.

Next to him a skipper asked, 'What's the matter, comrade? A louse run over your liver?' He chuckled.

Christian nodded, thinking that this was the third time he had heard that name 'Century'; first from the Big Lion, and then from poor old Trainburster Thomas whose bones were undoubtedly whitening in the sun now on that remote beach; now here again. 'Yes, something like that,' he answered suddenly subdued. '*A louse — with size-ten hobnail boots…*'

'Oskar, *you*!' Christian exclaimed in delight, thrusting out his right hand happily and then withdrawing it a little embarrassed as he realized that *Kapitänleutnant* Oskar von Hartstein's own right hand and most of the arm, too, had long vanished.

'Oh, don't frig around,' Flipper said heartily and put out his left hand. 'As long as you've got one hand to touch it and put in yer salami with, the girls are happy anyway. Christian, old house, what a pleasure to see you again after all these years!' He beamed and Christian noticed that although his old crewmate who had gone to war with him back in '39 as an officer-cadet was exactly the same age as himself, he was already grey. Flipper's war had been tough, that was obvious.

They shook hands awkwardly and began to walk to the docks, where at last the great secret was to be revealed to Christian, Oskar relating how he had lost his arm and had been dubbed 'Flipper' by no less a person than the Big Lion himself, and how he had refused to be pensioned off but had demanded — and received — a training job here in Danzig. 'It's not like combat, Christian,' he said, nodding to the helmeted sentries who saluted as the two veterans passed, 'but it's better any day than sitting in some office, ironing your arse fat and hoping that one of the office mattresses is going to let 'em down for you on Saturday night, as the big event of the war. *No sir*! Even training duffers like you is better than that.'

Flipper laughed and Christian laughed, too, and was surprised at himself for doing so. Suddenly he realized that he hadn't laughed for months, perhaps even years, for all he knew. Arm-in-arm, laughing like the cadets they had once been in another age, they walked inside the dockyard, ignoring the looks of the guards…

Everywhere there was noise and hectic bustle. The discordant rattle of cranes and derricks; the insane nerve-wracking chatter of the riveters' guns; the works super-intendants, self-important and red-faced, hurrying back and forth with their clipboards, stumbling and cursing as they tripped over the pipes and cables which were everywhere.

It was years since Christian had seen such activity. In the great ports of northern Germany — Hamburg, Bremen, Bremerhaven and the like — as well as those used by the *Kriegsmarine* in France — Brest, Cherbourg and Lorient — activity like this would immediately have attracted the Ami daylight bombers and they would have been followed at night by the RAF. 'Holy strawsack, Flipper,' Christian could not contain his surprise, 'you're living behind the moon here! I bet you don't even know what the word air-raid means?'

Flipper nodded happily. 'That's why the Big Lion picked Danzig for Project Tiger, Christian. So far, not one single enemy plane has ever been sighted within fifty kilometres of here.'

'Project Tiger?' Christian began, but Flipper stopped him with a proud, almost boastful, cry of, 'There she is, Christian - *Century One*...! And a little bird has told me she's going to be yours soon, you lucky bastard!'

Christian stopped. Beyond the barbed-wire, patrolled by guards carrying fixed bayonets, at the end of the glistening quay, there lay a submarine, shining new in its grey paint, looking like every other new U-boat straight from the shipyards that Christian had ever seen, save for one thing. The superstructure was dominated by a tall mast that he could not quite place. It wasn't anything to do with the radio, radar, or periscope. It was a piece of equipment completely beyond his ken.

Flipper followed the direction of his gaze and said, 'The snort, Christian. You're looking at the celebrated snort.'

'*Snort?*' Christian echoed. 'What in three devils' name is that?'

Flipper grinned cheekily. 'Oh, just the little piece of new gear some genius in Berlin invented which Big Lion thinks is going to win the war for our beloved Fatherland.' He lowered his cynical eyes in mock solemnity. 'Amen!'

But Christian was too intrigued for jokes or Flipper's kind of play-acting. '*Los*,' he commanded, '*heraus mit der Sprache*, what is it?'

'The Cheeseheads — Dutch to you — first tried it out back in 1940,' he said tantalizingly. 'They looked upon it just as a kind of air intake and only used it to ventilate their subs. German genius had to come along and transform it into a winner.'

'For Chrissake,' Christian almost bellowed at his old comrade, '*what is it?*'

'Your official designation for it is the *Schnorchel*,' Flipper answered easily, 'and it is in essence a retractable mast with a float — the *Schnorchel* — attached to it. This float allows the boat to take in fresh air all the time, charge the electric batteries while at sea.' He paused momentarily. 'And perhaps most important, allows its skipper to use the diesels underwater.'

Christian gasped and stopped as the full impact of those words hit.

'Yes,' Flipper nodded his head solemnly, 'it's true. A skipper raises his boat to, say, fourteen metres, still pretty deep, and opens the valves. The snort draws in fresh air. Naturally there can be problem. The snort does trail a white plume of foam behind it and if a skipper isn't careful, it can let off black smoke from the diesels…' His voice trailed away to nothing, as he saw that Christian wasn't listening.

For a moment there was no sound save the chattering of the riveters' hammers and a bored dockie's voice saying, 'And the arse-with-ears has the frigging cheek to say to me, there'll be no overtime for you on this, Heinemann. We've all got to do our bit for final victory. So I told him right sharpish where to stick his final victory!'

Suddenly Christian said, voice tense as the full import of what he had just heard struck him, 'So that means that with this new snort of yours, the Century class can sail underwater at full speed?'

Flipper nodded enthusiastically.

'And that means...' Suddenly Christian remembered Trainburster Thomas on board the *Puerto de Barcelona* on that bakingly hot day in the Indian Ocean. What had he said then in that slow, miserable manner of his? 'One of those Century class subs could sail round the world soon — and never surface once... A skipper would never need to go up topside until his fuel ran out.'

'Exactly, old house,' Flipper answered quite calmly, as if he were discussing the state of the weather and not the most revolutionary advance in the whole history of the submarine. 'Undoubtedly we'll have some joker trying to cross the whole of the Atlantic under water soon in an attempt to win himself a nice piece of tin, perhaps even the whole world.' He shrugged easily, while Christian's mind raced electrically.

Finally he stuttered, a new confidence and hope surging through his body, 'With a weapon like the Century class we might even win the war after all, Flipper!'

'Very probably, very probably indeed, old house,' Flipper said like a mother trying to soothe an overexcited child. He linked his one arm with Christian's once again and urged him forward. 'Come on, now,' he said, 'let old Flipper show you your new command, *Kapitänleutnant* Jungblut.'

In a complete daze Christian allowed himself to be led forward to that gleaming new boat, Century One ... the war-winner...

CHAPTER 3

Slowly the train from Danzig began to steam into the platform crowded with morose, pale-faced infantrymen returning to the front in Russia and their sobbing, miserable girlfriends and wives, watched on all sides by hard-eyed, helmeted Military Police ready to stamp out any sign of trouble.

High above them in the bomb-shattered roof, the loudspeakers crackled into soulless metallic life; 'Special troop-train to Königsberg, with connections to Warsaw, Brest-Litovsk… Planned departure ten hundred hours…'

The soldiers began wearily to sling their rifles and pick up their packs, engulfed in steam and smoke, as it rose sadly from the locomotive, turning them into grey wavering ghosts. The women started to sob even more, crying with mounting hysteria, 'Good-bye Karl… Good luck Heinz… Take care of yourself, sweet one… God speed…'

Normally these wartime stations with their sadness, their tears, their partings, depressed Christian. But not this fine winter's morning, with the sun shining over a battered, but bright Berlin. After what he had seen in Danzig, he felt confident and sure as he had never felt since the old days of victory after victory. Soon, with a bit of luck, Century One — and all the other boats of the Century class which were beginning to come out of the shipyards — would ensure that these tearful partings would be over for good.

Confidently he pushed his way through the sad, shabby crowd and showed his pass to the chain-dogs who clicked to attention and saluted smartly. Casually he returned their salute and stepped out into the keen air that always seemed to make

Berlin so alive, so vigorous. For an instant he looked around at the thronged street. Officers, self-important and smart, briefcases under their arms, obviously heading for one of the many ministries. Shabby workmen, yellow-faced and undernourished, coming off night-shift, dragging each foot as if it were a lead weight. Elegant women stepping down from the wood-burning taxis, which towed what looked like old stoves on the trailer behind them; whores or senior officers' wives, he concluded, or perhaps both. Ragged urchins searching the gutters for shrapnel from the previous night's raid. Pretty Hitler Maidens in white blouses and too-short skirts collecting marks for the 'Winter Help'. The whole busy, sad kaleidoscope of the capital of the Reich at war, in the year of 1944.

But it wasn't the street which really interested *Kapitänleutnant* Christian Jungblut, nor the elegant if somewhat cheap-looking woman who had just descended from one of the ancient taxis and was now eyeing him with undisguised interest. '*Where in three de* —' he began angrily.

And then there it was! There was no mistaking that drunken Hamburg voice as it bellowed cynically, '*Should we sink to the ocean floor, we still shall walk to the nearest shore. To you — Lilli Marlene... To you — my love!*'

Christian swung round. It was Frenssen all right. Oblivious to the gaping civilians and the red-faced officers, *Obermaat* Frenssen was staggering down the pavement, one foot in the gutter, his face unshaven, his jacket torn, and what looked like egg-yolk trickling down the breast. As for his Knight's Cross, which was the only thing which prevented him from being arrested by the fuming chain-dogs, it was back to front, hanging precariously over his shoulder.

Frenssen's red face lit up when he saw the skipper. He hobbled more quickly, crying, 'Sorry I'm late, sir. It's this frigging limp. Must be rheumatics or something — or too much mattress polka'ing. I didn't have it last night.' He threw Christian a tremendous salute — and missed his forehead completely! He would have fallen over if Christian hadn't caught him swiftly, hissing urgently, as a pompous-looking general staff officer marched by, tut-tutting angrily, 'Pull yourself together, you big rogue! You're a disgrace to the *Kriegsmarine*. *Himmel herrje*, where have you been? You *were* supposed to take care of the new crew, you know.'

'On patrol, sir,' Frenssen said happily and attempted the salute once more. This time he nearly made it.

'On patrol?'

'Yessir. I didn't want those greenbeaks of ours to suffer any kind of social disease — pox to you, sir — during their recreation period here in the big city... Between you and me, most of them don't look as if they know what it's meant for ... so I decided to do a personal reconn —' he hiccupped and said thickly, his mouth suddenly full of bitter bile, 'Do a personal recce of the *puffs* mesen!'

'Hm,' Christian said, not knowing whether to be angry or laugh, 'I see. I'm sure that you did a very thorough job, too.'

Frenssen took out a pair of red frilly knickers and mopped his brow. 'Yessir, Frau Frenssen's handsome son isn't one to let down the Submarine Service.' He grinned wickedly. 'Forty-eight hours solid, I've been on the nest, sir. *Forty-eight hours*! I bet the German rubber industry will have to work overtime to make up for what I've used in bed these last two days!'

'I bet,' Christian said sourly. 'All right, now pull yourself together and let's have a look at them.'

Frenssen stared down at his right foot in the gutter and frowned, as if he were puzzled how it came to be there, and then dismissed it with a doleful, 'You'll be sorry, sir, you'll be sorry...'

'All right, you heroes,' Frenssen commanded, a little more sober now, 'stand at ease!'

Christian stared at his new crew, his officers equally as young and inexperienced standing in a group behind him, running his gaze along the line. He took his time, almost as if he were trying to impress each individual face on his mind's eye. It was an old trick, he told himself, one that he had used three times now. Where were those other young faces? he asked himself, and then dismissed the question immediately. 'Soldiers — comrades,' he started slowly, still running his gaze down their ranks and telling himself how young the crew were. Some of them could not have been more than eighteen. 'You have been selected by the Admiral in charge of the U-boat Weapon for a key mission, I know that definitely, but at the present I do not know what it is exactly. But what I *do* know,' his voice rose and he smiled at them, 'is that you — we — have been granted the immense gift of a new secret, war-winning weapon!'

There was a gasp of surprise from the officers behind him and he could tell from the looks on his sailors' faces that they were surprised, too.

'I can't tell you very much about it at the moment, save this. Soon we shall sail in a revolutionary new craft, which is virtually *undetectable*! One that, even with the most modern and sophisticated apparatus, the enemy will be unable to find.' He let his own enthusiasm break through the rigid front that any captain had to put up in the presence of a new, impressionable crew. 'Comrades, when we sail to battle, we shall be sailing *in the most advanced submarine known to the world!*'

Carried away by the skipper's enthusiasm, Carlsen, the Leading Engineer, the only other old hare in the whole crew, cried, 'Three cheers for the captain. *Hip, hip!*'

But before the excited crew could burst into the cheer, the skinny bespectacled clerk who looked after the 'Sailors Home' thrust his head round the door and cried in alarm, 'It's the alert! The Amis are on their way to Berlin. Just heard it over the radio. It's the alert — *eight hundred of them...*' And with that he was gone, scuttling to the shelters below, no doubt...

Now the sirens started to wail the 'all clear' at last. To the west the majestic silver giants that had brought death and destruction from so far began to depart, followed by the angry flak. Here and there black-painted fighters, out of the range of the guns, streaked across the brown-pocked sky, their cannon chattering frantically. Slowly, almost imperviously, the Fortresses closed ranks, filling in the gaps they had suffered, forming gleaming boxes from which fire spat in all directions.

Frenssen, completely sober now, patted the dust from his blue uniform and grunted angrily, 'Look at the fat swine! Back now for bacon and eggs and a roll in the hay with some Tommy piece of gash! He spat into the smoking rubble. 'How big they think themselves, the gentlemen Americans, able to do this to us and get away with it, without even a frigging black eye!' He spat again, as more and more of Christian's new crew began to creep out of the shelter and stare in awe at the scene before them.

As a burning roof opposite slithered down in a shower of angry red sparks, making them jump with surprise, the first of the refugees began leaving the shattered city. Many of them were naked and barefoot, their skinny bodies smeared with soot and blood. The newly blind were led by the others holding brooms. Others were pushed by their weeping relatives in prams or barrows like grotesque, scarlet babies.

Christian frowned and together with Frenssen crossed the smoking, brick-littered street to where a woman lay, skirts raised obscenely, body crumpled in an unnatural position.

But she was already dead and the naked baby she cradled lovingly in her dead arms was, too. Gravely he bent down and closed her eyelids. Frenssen took off his jacket and without a word covered the naked baby with it, as if it were important.

Now more and more civilians were streaming out of the capital, heading for the fields and woods beyond. They might freeze or starve out there, but at least they would not be torn apart so cruelly by the RAF bombers when they came this night, as they surely would, to finish the terrible work of destruction begun by the Amis.

Christian's anger grew by the instant. What purpose did it serve to kill and terrorize these poor, downtrodden civilians? Would it shorten the war by one second, bring an Allied victory any closer? he asked himself, fists clenched in impotent fury.

Now they were limping by him. Children sobbing with fear, hopping along on their wounded legs like little human rabbits. Women, eyes bulging out of their ashen faces under newly-white hair, screaming silently, mad, completely mad. Old men coughing and coughing with the smoke and gases, as if their very lungs might burst at any moment. And the carts, drawn by the ancient nags, laden high with their freight of death; men, women and children shrunken to the size of pygmies; human trunks without heads, arms or legs; horror after horror. As Christian gazed at this doleful procession, it seemed to him like some medieval wood-cut of the victims of the Black Death, terror-stricken, hopeless, trying futilely to escape from a skeletal Grim Reaper from whom there was no reprieve.

He turned, sickened, unable to stand it any longer. He swung round on Frenssen. 'Assemble the crew, *Obermaat*,' he commanded angrily, 'we leave for Brest this very night. *At the double now!*' But as Frenssen moved away, suddenly sullen, to carry out the skipper's order, Christian glared at that burning sky and made a solemn promise to himself, his eyes filled with a burning hatred; 'You'll pay,' he hissed, '*by God, you'll pay tenfold for this!*' His face hollowed out to a crimson death's head by the flames opposite, he pressed his hand to his heart, as if he were making a binding, unbreakable covenant with himself...

CHAPTER 4

Savage took up his big binoculars.

Now the tank-landing craft were in position around the British destroyers which were to play the role of their escort in the landing exercise to come. The sea, at least, was calm, the grey mournful waves sliding back and forth smoothly enough. But the ugly grey landing craft were not meant for even a swell such as this and he could well imagine his soldiers being sick into their helmet liners as usual.

Around him in his own craft, the headquarters staff tensed. Already the signallers had netted their radios and the two dispatch riders were revving up their bikes like highly strung thoroughbreds at the starting gate, impatient to be off. Savage sensed, too, Peewee standing just behind him, hand on the holster of that big forty-five he wore all the time these days. He gave a wry grin. If the Germans didn't get him, he told himself, Peewee would.

From the biggest of the destroyers, which was Buck's floating HQ, a green flare sailed high into the dull grey sky and hung there for a few flickering moments before it came floating down like a fallen angel. It was the signal.

Almost at once, all hell broke loose. The rocket barges opened up with a tremendous roar. A flight of scarlet rockets flew into the sky, hesitated, and came soaring down to the beach like a swarm of angry red hornets. Mustangs started screaming in, dozens of them, at mast-top height. Below, the soldiers packed in the barges ducked their heads like frightened tortoises. Ship whistles shrilled. Rattles turned.

Officers and red-faced noncoms yelled angry orders. Cranes and anchor chains rattled rustily.

Suddenly the motors of the barges and the landing craft burst into noisy, frantic life. Savage dropped his glasses. They were moving at last. Behind him Peewee yelled exuberantly, 'Goddammit to all hell, Colonel, sir! *Ain't this something!*'

Savage didn't reply. His whole attention was focused on the first wave of barges, breasting the waves now, a white bone in their teeth, as they surged towards Slapton Sands. They carried his two leading assault companies. In the real thing, they would have to hit that beach, together with combat engineers, cutting and snapping at the wire, knocking out the 'Rommel asparagus', as it was called, in short; putting out of action the hundred and one lethal devices Intelligence told them the Germans had planted over there on their beaches, so that the Shermans could roll up the sand. Then in those final moments, when the naval bombardment lifted so as not to hit their own men, the only artillery he would possess would be those 75mm cannon of the Shermans.

Now the barges were swarming up to the beach in fine style. Savage, without taking his eyes off them, yelled above the crazy racket to the young skipper of his own craft, an eighteen-year-old British sub-lieutenant, 'Okay, Nelson, take her away!'

The young 'snotty' grinned and did just that. They began to race for the beach. Behind Savage, Peewee drew his forty-five as Colonel Lanham had ordered him to do, his eyes fixed hard on the small of the tall lean battalion commander's back.

Now the first landing barges were hitting the beach. A flurry of wild, white water. The harsh grating of the gravel. Suddenly the ramps were creaking down and the soldiers, carried away by the excitement and noise of it all, were rushing out cheering wildly, swinging alternatively to left and right as they had been taught. Up on the heights the marksmen opened fire with their machine guns. Live slugs ripped the length of beach in front of them. Little spurts of sand zipped across their lines. Still the young men of Savage's battalion didn't hesitate. They went charging in, throwing themselves across the coils of barbed wire in fine style, while the combat engineers, laden with their long explosive torpedo tubes, doubled furiously after them, ready to blow the more serious obstacles.

Savage nodded his head with satisfaction and swung his glasses round to the ponderous tank-landing ships, wallowing heavily in the shallows. He cursed. The leading wave had already hit the beach and there was still no sign of the leading waterproof tanks. He yelled to the nearest radio operator, 'Charley, get on to those damned landing craft and tell 'em to get the lead outa their asses! *Pronto!*'

'*Sir!*' the operator yelled back.

Savage spared a glance for the members of his own barge, as its blunt bows struck the sea time and time again with a stomach-churning thud as if it were hitting a solid brick wall. The soldiers, crouched there behind the steel plating, looked so young and so excited, like kids on some summer camp adventure. Did they realize, as the salt water came over the bows and showered them, that in a few weeks or months this would be for real; that it was a deadly game from which a lot of them wouldn't return? But if they did, their faces gave little evidence of it. Most of them chewed gum stolidly.

Gunfire pounded the beach now, interspersed with the screech of the rockets. Everywhere huge brown steaming holes had opened like the work of giant moles. Smoke drifted on all sides, obscuring the little figures busily working their way through the obstacles, as if they had been whipped away for all time, only to reappear a few moments later as determined and as purposeful as ever.

Savage allowed himself a thin smile. Things were going well. The little colonel would be pleased. All the intensive new training had begun to pay dividends. His boys had the same kind of dash his old troopers of the US Third Infantry Division had had once back in 1942 before they had become jaded, war-weary and cynical. He looked back over his shoulder at the anxious freckled little Texan and his big gun. 'Don't think you're gonna have to use that cannon on me —'

There was a tremendous crash to his front. A quiver of rockets seared out of the burning sky and struck the beach a thunderous blow. In an instant, all was noise, confusion and wailing, as khaki-clad bodies were flung everywhere in a gory mess of flailing, flying limbs. A shocked, suddenly ashen-faced Savage caught a frightening glimpse of a head, complete with helmet, rolling along the beach and then the fog of war descended on that scene of horror and he knew one of those pointless tragedies of war had occurred yet once again...

The woman looked at him across the lounge and he knew from the way she did so that she knew he was drunk, almost gone; an American colonel of infantry, with two years of combat experience behind him, drunk in a public place. But he didn't care.

Twenty killed; that had been the final toll — and twice that number seriously wounded, some of them, according to the limey doctors in Exeter, not expected to live till the morning. Twenty or thirty young Americans killed even before they had started to live, killed for nothing. Their sudden deaths had served not even to warn the others. Some bastard on the rocket ship had make a mistake in elementary maths and that

135

was that. There wouldn't even be an official inquiry. 'Fortunes of war,' the admiral had said, according to Buck. 'You can't make an omelette without breaking eggs.'

He had told Buck what the 'fucking Admiral' could do with his 'fucking eggs' and had gone off to get drunk. Now he was here in this olde worlde English pub, which looked as if it had come straight from the set of Hollywood's *Mrs Minniver*, packed with officers in khaki and olive drab, and the woman was looking at him, knowing, in spite of his pose, the small glass of beer on the table in front of him, that he was drunk — and he still didn't care.

The woman smiled. He considered. She had a fleshy, mobile body, not very English, more like the women he had frequented when they had come back from the front in Messina and Bari. Perhaps she was a foreigner, a spy. He looked around, almost as if he half expected Peewee with his forty-five to be lurking there in the potted palms, next to the gleaming dinner-gong. He wasn't. He was safe. He made a decision. He smiled back.

The woman took her time.

She uncrossed her legs deliberately and slowly. He caught a glimpse of the plump white flesh above the black stockings. As drunk as he was he felt excited. Taking a long steady look at him, as if she were making an important decision of some kind, she rose and came across to him. Her face serious, with none of those fake professional smiles he had come to know from the whores, the only women available to a combat soldier, she said; 'You don't look particularly happy, and drink won't make it any better.'

He rose unsteadily and said, 'Won't you sit down please?'

'No,' she said quite firmly. 'I only came here to meet someone … like you.' She indicated the hotel bar. 'If you really need some more to drink, you can ask Freddie; the tall one. For a fiver and a ten bob tip, he'll sell you a bottle of black market scotch or gin. 'Go on,' she urged, after a moment, when he didn't move.

'But where are we going?' he asked puzzled.

'Home, to my house,' she answered, those dark eyes of hers still unsmiling. '*Please.*' And there was no mistaking that note of pleading in her voice.

Colonel Savage nodded. 'I think I'll see what Freddie can sell me,' he said thickly. 'Don't run away.'

'I won't,' she answered solemnly...

'You married, Sam?' she asked and kissed him again before he could even answer, as he sat there on the overstuffed settee in that big dark cold room, the last few embers of coal slowly going out in the Victorian grate.

'*Was*! Before I went to North Africa. In '42. Got a Dear John just before we invaded Sicily.' He shrugged. 'Suppose it had to happen.'

'Dear John?' She moved his glass closer to him.

He didn't touch it. 'A letter saying she was sorry ... met another guy. That sort of thing. You?'

In the hall the grandfather clock chimed midnight. All was silent. The big old house echoed to the chimes sadly. They might well have been the last people alive in the whole world.

'*Was*! Till '42.' She aped his speech. 'Got a telegram from the War Department. Killed at El Alamein. Drink!'

He drank. 'A bitch, eh?'

'A bitch,' she echoed and smiled at him carefully. 'Still unhappy, Sam?'

He thought for a moment, seriously. He thought of that damned salvo of rockets and their torn, dismembered young bodies, and the letters he had written that afternoon to their next-of-kin. He shook his head and looked down at his glass, a wry grin on his lean, bronzed face. 'No,' he answered, 'and I don't think I'm even drunk anymore, either. How's that?'

She grinned, too, in that careful way of hers, as if she had learned to keep her emotions well under control, just as he had. 'Well, that's progress, isn't it ... for the class of '42?'

'Yeah, I guess it is, *for the class of '42*!' He took a sip of the scotch and told himself he didn't need it anymore. He had gotten over the tragedy. The woman was good for him. 'You want me to stay?'

'Of course, Sam, what a damn fool question! You're my Saturday night treat.' She grinned, as if at some private joke. 'It goes with a Saturday night bath and a change of underclothes. There are precious few treats around for the class of '42.' She leaned over and kissed him on the cheek, gently.

'Do you give yourself many Saturday night treats?' he asked carefully.

'Not often. As my butcher used to say before he went away in '39, "Don't give him steak every day, missus, or he'll stop appreciating it." ' She mimicked the local Devon accent perfectly and he knew who 'he' was — *had been*, he corrected himself mentally.

'Well, I haven't been compared with steak before,' he said, noting how the nipples of her ample breasts had become erect beneath the thin material of her dress. She was excited, *or cold*! 'Shall we go to bed, May?'

'Naturally,' she said eagerly. 'I've been waiting for the last hour for you to damn well ask me...'

Later she lay awake, staring at him in the cold moonlight that came through a chink in the black-out curtain. He lay on the rumpled pillow, eyes closed, no movement in that sad, scarred soldier's face of his. He hardly seemed to be breathing. She frowned. For all she knew, he might well already be dead…

CHAPTER 5

'Close the doors now, we're all here,' the Big Lion snapped in that harsh, tight-lipped manner of his.

The two helmeted petty officers, with carbines slung over their shoulders, clicked to attention, saluted and closed the big double doors of the conference room in the former French Naval Academy in Brest which now housed the First U-Boat Flotilla.

The Big Lion waited until they had done so and then barked to the assembled officers, 'Brest is a hot-bed of English espionage, *meine Herren*, we cannot be too careful. You may sit now. Smoke if you wish.'

There was a soft murmur of chatter. A few of the assembled officers coughed. A scraping of chairs. Even the E-boat officers, mostly pale-faced second lieutenants in their teens, were awed by the presence of Admiral Dönitz, the Big Lion. Christian wasn't surprised. The Big Lion would awe even the Devil himself.

While the aides fiddled with the maps on the wall, Christian looked at the E-boat officers. All of them were exceedingly pale and he knew why. Most of their stomachs were ruined by the constant battering they suffered when their craft hit the waves at forty knots an hour; it was like hitting a series of solid brick walls. Just as submariners all ended up with rheumatics, if they lived long enough, the E-boat men were landed with ruined stomachs. He bet that most of them present here today lived off schnaps and baby food. But why were they here? What had the Big Lion got to do with E-boat officers? And for that matter why had he been summoned here so hastily with his new crew? He had not even had the chance to shake them down in his new command, 'Century One', wherever the revolutionary U-boat might be at this particular moment.

But after five years of total war Christian Jungblut had become accustomed to the whims and vagaries of the High Command. So he bided his time, wondering whether this 'hot-bed of English espionage' still served those tremendous lobster dinners down by the old port.

'*Meine Herren*, may I have your attention now please?' the Big Lion's harsh incisive voice cut into his reverie and he sat up sharply.

The Big Lion, his flat, bitter-mouthed face set and hard, was standing ram-rod straight in front of the big map of the English Channel tensely, pointer held in his hands as if it were a deadly weapon.

'*Here*,' he tapped the chart, 'the army of General Patton.' '*Here,*' he tapped it again in the south-west, 'the army of General Bradley! Both preparing for an attack on our Atlantic Wall and the invasion of France. The question puzzling us is, naturally, where those two armies will attack, for the enemy has only sufficient strength for an attack in one spot. Will it be here, at Calais, as some of our experts think? Or here further south, at the tip of the Normandy Peninsula?' He paused to let his words sink in.

Outside, the seagulls swooped and swerved, crying like abandoned children. In the fog-bound estuary a boat hooted mournfully. Suddenly Christian shivered and told himself it must be this grey drab day which caused him to do so.

'Now, *meine Herren*,' the Big Lion rasped, 'in these last few months, our agents in England have learned several things about the plans of the Anglo-American air gangsters which might help us to solve the great mystery; where they are going to attack us this summer?' He tapped the chart in the area of Scotland. 'Up here, the English are training their assault troops for the attack, and down here,' he tapped the south coast, 'the Americans are doing the same thing, at a place named Slapton.' He took a deep breath. 'Scotland for our purposes is quite out of the question. It is too far from our bases and too well protected by the English Home Fleet. So we are left with Slapton in their county of Devon.'

'Are we now?' one of the young E-boat skippers whispered cheekily to one of his comrades out of the side of his mouth. 'Left to do what with it?'

'Shut up, Otto!' his comrade hissed warningly. 'He's got his beady little orbits on us already.' Christian grinned. At least somebody in the hard-pressed *Kriegsmarine* seemed happy in this bad winter of 1944.

'Now,' the Big Lion continued, 'we have learned something else about their invasion plans from our agents. One of them, who I had wished to be here for this briefing today, has apparently died of gunshot wounds in Dublin.'

Dönitz frowned and the E-boat skipper named Otto whispered, 'Oh, how very naughty of him to do so!'

'Anyway, this dead agent has reported that, although he could not penetrate the American training ground at Slapton, he had learned that there were officers always present there during their training exercises who knew *where the real landings will take place on the day*! These officers are code-named Bigots, for some reason known only to the crazy Anglo-Saxons.'

Dönitz paused and let his audience absorb the information. Christian frowned and wondered where all this was leading. What had this mixed group of E- and U-boat skippers got to do with enemy code-names and training exercises?

The Big Lion enlightened him the next moment. 'Now if it were possible — how shall I put it? — to obtain one of these Bigot officers alive, we would know in advance where the enemy would attack, and I have been assured by no less a person than Field Marshal Rommel himself that they will be unable to change their plans for this year. If they wish to attack the Atlantic Wall in 1944, it must be in the area they have already decided upon.'

'So, *Herr Admiral*,' the skipper named Otto said cheekily, 'why haven't our Intelligence people tried to nobble a — er — Bigot by now?'

The Big Lion shot the pale-faced E-boat skipper a murderous glance and his aides looked shocked. No U-boat skipper, even the greatest sub aces, would have dared to interrupt the Big Lion when he was giving a briefing. It was almost like breaking into a pronouncement by God himself!

'I can assure you, young man, that the matter has already been discussed at the highest level,' the Big Lion said icily. 'The Army says it cannot mount a commando raid against the British coast to capture one of these Bigots, and *Obersturmbannführer* Skorzeny, the head of the SS's own commandos, maintains an airborne raid such as he carried out last October to rescue Signor Mussolini from his place of imprisonment is out of the question. It is barely possible for our fastest fighter planes to penetrate English air-space, let alone a para-troop transport. So, gentlemen, it has been left to the *Kriegsmarine* to make the attempt.' He gazed around at their suddenly shocked faces. '*Meine Herren*, before this month is out, we will take one of these Bigots prisoner and undoubtedly win the war for our beloved Fatherland!'

Christian Jungblut walked out of the former French Naval College in a state of shock, not even acknowledging the salutes of the sentries, hard-eyed and heavily armed, who were everywhere. A self-important staff officer snapped something at him angrily. Christian did not seem to hear; for his mind was racing, totally pre-occupied with what he had just been told. *'Mission impossible, but it will be done,'* the Big Lion had rasped at the end of his long briefing; and it did seem that their new mission was impossible. Yet, with a bit of luck it *could* succeed! He knew it could. Suddenly Christian found himself clenching his fists, as if he were angry. He forced himself to relax and try to contain his racing thoughts, as he walked down the port's picturesque streets between the bistros, cafés and shops, all doing thriving business, selling their wares to the Germans who were everywhere, including the whores who seemed to lounge provocatively at every corner.

But this day Christian had no time for lobster dinners or the very seductive wares, however tempting, of the whores. He knew he must round up his crew and begin his planning before the Century One arrived in that strange fashion in which the Big Lion had told him it would be delivered to Brest. 'Holy strawsack,' he cursed softly to himself as he headed for the coastal village, with its superb view of the harbour and the Crozon Peninsula where the crew were housed, *'imagine having a U-boat delivered by rail.'*

'What did you say, sir?' Carlsen, the LE, exclaimed when he told them, 'Century One's coming cross-country by train?'

Christian grinned, pleased with his surprise. 'Exactly, courtesy of the *Reichsbahn*. The Big Lion is taking no chances. He will not risk having the Tommies attack it in the shallow waters of the exit to the Baltic. Nor will he have its security compromised by allowing it to sail from Danzig. There are plenty of Poles in the area who might well be reporting to London.'

'But how are they going to transport the tin can by rail?' Frenssen objected.

'Tin can, indeed. *Tut tut!*' Christian chided him mildly. 'Please, *Herr Obermaat*, show a little more respect, will you, for this war-winning product of German genius!'

Frenssen muttered something about sticking 'German genius' in an impossible place and relapsed into a red-faced silence.

'How are they going to transport it?' Christian answered his own question. 'In Danzig they are going to divide Century One into three sections, which will be reassembled here by a special crew of riggers and fitters who will travel with the transport from Danzig. This whole thing is so hot that the Big Lion has ordered that none of the French workers we usually employ here in Brest will be used on the job. It will be a strictly one hundred percent German affair. The fewer people, French or otherwise, who know about 'Project Tiger', as this operation is code-named, the better.'

'But sir,' Carlsen said, obviously expressing the views of all the crew, 'say we get the Century One here in this funny way and we receive the new super torpedoes the Big Lion has promised us...' he hesitated momentarily, red-faced and not a little puzzled, '...what then? What are we going to do with them and the boat? Are we going to operate in the English Channel against their invasion fleet, once they finally decide to attack us?'

Christian bit his bottom lip. He didn't like to lie to the men, who soon would be risking their lives under his command to carry out 'Project Tiger'. But the Big Lion had sworn all of the skippers present at that key briefing to the utmost secrecy. Indeed he had forced all of them to sign a document stating exactly that. Now if anyone babbled it would be a matter for the Gestapo and the hangman in his frock-coat and top-hat. So he lied; 'Something like that, you could say.' At that moment he caught the look on Frenssen's face and it said all too clearly, 'You're damn well lying, Christian Jungblut!' So he said, hurriedly, to cover his own embarrassment, feeling himself flush like some nervous youngster seeing what a woman had between her legs for the very first time. 'Now, comrades, we have got a great deal to do in the next few days. Firstly we're moving out across the bay to Camaret, away from Brest. There are too many prying eyes there and too many charming little French girls asking leading questions for us to carry out what we're going to do.'

Frenssen moaned out loud. 'War *is* hell! It does get in the way of a sailor's sex life!'

Nobody laughed. They were all too intent on Christian's explanation for their surprise move.

'You see, there is an old dry-dock there, not protected, like the underground ones in Brest, against Allied air attacks, but one they have never yet made an attack upon. Besides, when we finally sail there will be no one there to tip the Tommies off we're leaving, as there always is in Brest.'

'You mean, sir, that that is where they are going to reassemble Century One?' Carlsen asked.

Christian nodded.

'I know the area, sir. It's pretty lonely. I mean if the French Resistance did decide to try something —'

Frenssen farted contemptuously and pulled a face.

But the Leading Engineer persisted. 'If they did, it would be an ideal spot for them to attack us. There isn't a German garrison within twenty kilometres, the road network is limited to a couple of D-roads, and Brest is way across the estuary.' He ended a little lamely, 'We'd be out on a limb over there.'

'I know it,' Christian answered hastily, not wanting to frighten his young crew, who obviously had already heard some horrific stories about the Resistance, how they had the habit of knifing lone German sailors or even emasculating them if they found them with French girls, however willing. 'The Big Lion has taken that into consideration. From this day onwards every man in the crew will never move out of his billet — *even for a piss* — without being armed. Our own security is now in our own hands, and more importantly, comrades,' Christian looked around at their honest young faces, 'that of the Century One is, too. Once the rail transport leaves the main line from Paris at Morlaix and starts moving south-west to Camaret, we are responsible for the boat's safety. And remember this, comrades, although I can't tell you all the details of our mission yet, you can rest assured that it is not going to be just another combat cruise, knocking off a few enemy merchant ships. This one might well help to end the war in Germany's favour.' Christian wasted no more time and he wanted no more questions either. Putting his battered white cap firmly on his cropped blond head, he snapped, '*Obermaat* Frenssen, dismiss the men!'

The big noncom looked for a moment as if he might refuse the order, then he bellowed it out and they clicked to attention as Christian stepped out into the cold afternoon, his mind full of the great plan.

CHAPTER 6

As the winter of that fateful year of 1944 gave way to the spring, Colonel Savage began to like his new battalion. Their days were full of searing sea-winds, bellowed commands and unrelieved strain which had his young men gasping from lungs which sounded like broken bellows, limbs trembling, broken only by hasty meals snatched out of little khaki-painted cans.

Their nights were little different. For Savage, training did not cease when the light went. Time and time again, he and his noncoms would toss thunder-flashes through the open windows of their huts or through the flaps of their tents, yelling 'Surprise attack … surprise attack! Stand to everywhere!' And off they would be again, running half-dressed, half-asleep into the cold damp moors above the camp to attack the 'enemy'.

Only minutes later, or it seemed to the permanently exhausted soldiers of Savage's First Battalion, the harsh-voiced noncoms would be parading through their huts and tents, slapping the ends of their cots with pick-axe handles, yelling, 'Okay, you guys, let's be having it … hands off ya cocks and on with ya socks! *Move it!*' and another long exhausting day of training would begin.

But the ruthless, relentless training had begun to pay dividends, Savage could see that all right. Their puppy-fat had gone now. Now they were lean and hard, their eyes luminous in faces that had been hollowed out almost to death's heads. Now they were capable of going all day without food or water, carrying out the murderous training exercises in this lonely coastal area from which the local civilians had long been evacuated, with sixty pounds of equipment on their bent backs, the sweat streaming down their crimson faces.

The little colonel was impressed. 'You've worked wonders, Sam!' he congratulated Savage more than once. 'Before you came they were not much better than a bunch of canteen commandos. Now they're soldiers!' And invariably Savage would reply carefully, 'They're coming on, Buck. But the real proof of how good they are is when…' And he would leave the little colonel to complete the sentence with a sombre, 'When they come under fire for the first time…'

Eisenhower and the little limey Montgomery came down to see them again. Savage put on a cliff-assault exercise from the sea for the Top Brass. The ramp of the barges slapping against the wet pebbles. The crunch of their boots as they sprinted across the beach. The grapnels hitting and cutting into the top of the chalk cliff, towing a hundred feet of rope behind them. Excited, nervous men swarming up them like khaki-clad monkeys, while up above marksmen sprayed the turf with live ammunition. Then over the wire and charging forward, yelling their heads off straight into the smoke screen, bayonets fixed, to collapse at the end of it, chests heaving, crimson faces glazed with sweat, while the umpires fussed around, comparing their notes.

But the Top Brass had needed no umpire reports to make their assessment. Eisenhower had shaken Savage by the hand and had said, 'Swell, a swell exercise, Colonel! Train hard and fight easy.' Montgomery had had the whole battalion paraded and had walked their ranks, hawk-like eyes staring into each strained American face and in the end he had barked to Savage, 'And what's the average age of your men, Colonel?'

'Twenty-two, sir.'

The little Englishman had nodded his head sagely and said, almost to himself, 'A good age ... a good age for assault infantry...'

Of an evening he would watch them stagger back to their huts and tents, bodies shaking uncontrollably, as if they were in the throes of some tropical fever. But later when they had eaten and washed up, and they would take their last stroll before turning in, he felt a glow of pride in them; their young unlined faces now tanned and glowing with good health, their gestures quick and assured. Now there were no more canteen commandos, feather merchants, left in the First Battalion, he told himself.

But always there was Peewee lurking in the background, hand on holster of that big pistol he carried with him all the time (Savage suspected he might well sleep with it), sensed more than seen; for he was too busy to concern himself with the little Texan marksman during the day. At first Peewee had been a kind of macabre joke; then he had become a necessary nuisance; now he was a threat, a constant reminder of impending death.

'Christ, May,' he once exclaimed to the Englishwoman after spotting Peewee lurking in that same olde worlde hotel where they had first met and where he still bought his Saturday night bottle of black market whisky from the ever obliging Freddie, 'that guy's like a goddam monkey on my back! He's always hanging around. I swear, one of these days we'll wake up *and find the little creep in bed with us*!'

Once she had asked him, when he was drunk of a Saturday evening, why he was always so angry with the undersized Texan, and he had snorted, 'I'm not *angry* at the jerk, I'm damn well plain *scared* of him!'

'The class of '42 is scared of nothing!' she had said, attempting to laugh it off.

'Well, this member is. That guy's supposed to shoot me one day!' he had declared, suddenly moody and black-browed.

Again she had laughed in that careful way of hers and passed it off as another one of his bitter jokes of the kind he always made when he was drunk. But afterwards, when they had made love and he had fallen into the usual noiseless, exhausted sleep, she had stared at his lean, haggard face in the moonlight, worried. Finally she had stroked his forehead tenderly as a mother might do for a dearly loved child troubled by bad dreams, before turning and drifting finally off to sleep herself…

On the other side of the Channel, Christian too was under similar pressure, and worried as well. It was not only that the civilian technicians were taking a long time to reassemble the Century One, cutting ever more into the time he needed to train his raw crew to use the revolutionary new craft; it was their security, too. The rough, tough, middle-aged workmen from Germany's north coast took poorly to naval discipline. Christian suspected that most of them had been communists anyway before the Führer had taken over power in 1933 (their kind always had been traditionally). They simply refused to observe the curfew or go into the little towns and villages around the dry-docks in pairs and armed, as did his sailors. They slipped off to find women and drink when and where they pleased, shrugging off his warnings with a careless, 'Oh, don't you worry, *Herr Kapitänleutnant*, we from the Waterfront can take of ourselves, we don't want anyone fussing about us.' And a frustrated and angry Christian could see by the looks on their tough, unshaven workingmen's faces that they took him for some nervous nelly of a naval officer, who had no concept of how a real man lived.

'Can't you keep your glassy orbits on them, you big rogue?' Christian had once complained a little bitterly to Frenssen. 'If anybody knows the knocking shops and gin-mills around here, it's sure to be you!'

Frenssen had grinned in that lazy, good-humoured manner of his, wiped a paw like a small steam-shovel across his broad face, and had boomed; 'That I do, sir. That I do! But yer can't keep tabs on that lot! *It's like trying to keep a sailor's dong in his drawers on payday*! Just can't be done. They must be pleasuring half the widow women from here to Brest. They'll screw anything with hair, including the brooms.' He had shaken his head in mock wonder. 'No sir! Nobody can keep that lot of rampant roosters under control!'

Christian had had to give in on the civilians. Instead he had mounted a permanent guard of a petty officer and six men armed with submachine guns on Century One, obtaining the paymaster's permission to offer the civilian foremen a substantial bonus if they could get their men to finish the work on the U-boat so that he could get her to sea and away from the potential dangers of Camaret.

In the first week of the new spring, the courier from Dönitz's battle headquarters in the former French Naval College brought a top secret message from the Big Lion which lent even more urgency to his aim of getting to sea as soon as possible. Even in clear, after he had used the one-way pad to de-code it, it would have meant little to anyone who was not in on the great secret. For it read simply; '*Project Tiger to run 28.4.44. One hundred percent reliable source. Dönitz.*'

Sitting in his locked office, his pistol lying on the desk in front of him — just in case — Christian stared at the de-code.

In a moment he would destroy it, as he had been ordered to do. But for a moment he stared at it and savoured its full meaning. '*One hundred percent reliable source.*' He knew what that meant. At Mürwik they had been breaking the Royal Navy's top secret code for years now. That meant the decoders had broken an Admiralty command from London, ordering the convoy to sea on the 28th April 1944. Christian frowned and, clicking his lighter, applied the little blue flame to the sheet of paper. As it burned, the poor quality yellow wartime paper spluttering slowly, he told himself that he had just one more month left to take Century One to sea and shake his raw crew down for the great task ahead.

It seemed impossible. Four short weeks and Century One was not even sea-worthy yet! Still, as that terrible scene from Berlin after the air-raid flashed before his mind's eye once more, as it did a lot these days, he knew he could do it. *Must!* The Anglo-American air terrorists *had* to be paid back for the suffering they had caused back in the Reich. Almost savagely, hardly feeling the heat and pain, he crushed the glowing ember in his right hand and pulped it to black dust...

'*J'attendrais le jour et la nuit,*' the syrupy, sad woman's voice intoned out of the big radio next to the bar, as they sat there in the wicker chairs outside, enjoying the thin spring sunshine, '*j'attendrais toujours son retour...*'

Christian took a sip of his *pastis* and told himself whenever he thought about France in wartime in the future, if there was a future for him, he would always remember that sad little love song. It would invariably mean France for him.

Next to him Carlsen put down his glass of beer and said, '*Nice* arse, *nice* tits, *nice* legs. Pity I'm broke!' He nodded at the whore sauntering by the outdoor cafe, swaying her hips provocatively. He sighed. 'As always the course of true love for a poor old sailor man never runs smooth.' He grinned and Christian grinned, too, in spite of his worries.

'Four more days to payday, LE, and you can fall head over heels in love once more,' he said lazily, savouring the swish of the whore's tight little buttocks as she disappeared round the corner in search of customers, telling himself he hadn't had a woman himself since Danzig.

'Harvest the good life, sir,' Carlsen said, 'before death harvests us.'

'Dreary thoughts for a splendid day like this, LE,' Christian said lightly and clicked his fingers at the old waiter to bring fresh drinks. If he couldn't allow himself a woman in this dangerous place, at least he could afford to get a little drunk in safety.

Carlsen, the Leading Engineer, forgot the whore for a moment, and rubbed his horny hands together, the nails as always black with engine-grease, as if he were cold. 'Is it going to be a bad one, sir?' he asked.

'Bad what?' Christian asked, knowing full well what the LE meant. In a surly manner the old waiter put down their drinks, spilling Carlsen's beer a little. Christian told himself it was typical. Back in '40 when they had first come to Brest, the French had been all smiles for their conquerors. Now since Stalingrad and with the prospect of the Allies landing in France soon, things had changed dramatically. Now *les boches* were their bitter enemies once more. He dismissed the matter. It was not worth thinking about.

'Our next patrol, sir. You know, if you permit me to say so, sir, you can fool those greenbeaks, but not an old hare like myself. This is going to be a big one of some kind, isn't it, sir?' the LE persisted. 'And big ones can often result in the sharks eating up the little fish like us.'

Christian smiled at the old phrase. How long ago had it been since he was a 'little fish'. Now that was all behind him. So he said, 'Now come, come, LE, don't get morbid. We're all sharks these days. It's all that dirty water on your manly chest,' he joked, 'it's getting you down. You wait till payday comes along again and then you'll be your old self —'

He stopped short. *Obermaat* Frenssen, pistol at his belt, heavy sack over his shoulder, was marching smartly across the *place*, with two greenbeaks, both carrying carbines, trotting meekly behind him.

The LE whistled softly and Christian said, 'You know where that big rogue is heading for, don't you, LE?'

The LE nodded enviously. 'You don't need a crystal ball for that, sir. Madame Liz's celebrated *établissement*'

'Exactly,' Christian agreed, not knowing whether to be amused or angered. At least the big rogue was taking two armed guards with him to ensure his security while engaged in 'dancing the mattress polka,' as he would undoubtedly put it.

'But where's he got the green stuff at this time of the month?' the LE asked.

'Can't you guess, LE? That sack! I bet the big rogue has got half the dockies' cigarette ration or the like in there. Madame Liz has catholic tastes as regards payment.'

'And in other things, too,' the LE hinted darkly, finishing his beer. 'Have you seen the whips she's got hanging on the walls of her office?'

Christian nodded and finished his drink as well. He placed a wad of thin franc notes on the table, including a generous tip for the surly old waiter. 'Come on, LE, let's get back to the dock. Can't have the civvies see you with your tongue hanging out like that. It wouldn't do for the prestige of the *Kriegsmarine*.'

The LE took his envious gaze off Frenssen and his escort as they swung round the corner, obviously in a hurry. 'It isn't my *tongue* that's hanging out, skipper,' he said miserably and tugged on his cap. 'Roll on frigging payday.' But Leading Engineer Carlsen was not fated to see another payday; and behind them, the surly waiter spat on his tip and growled, '*Salaud.*' Then he hurried off to the telephone to make his report, as he had been ordered to; and a tense expectant mood began to settle on the isolated little port...

CHAPTER 7

'I'm dying ... dying on the job!' Frenssen had exclaimed in sheer delight — and had passed out cold.

Now his escort, the two young sailors in their teens, stood awkwardly near the bar, trying not to ogle the half-naked whores who were not shy of displaying their ample charms and who regarded the two blushing greenbeaks with amused, professional contempt.

Madame Liz, a fragile woman in her early thirties, with jet-black hair pulled back tightly from her forehead so that her eyes always seemed half-closed, as if she might be shortsighted, was neither amused nor worried that she had uninvited non-paying guests in her *établissement*. Her mind was still preoccupied with the waiter's phone call and the one she had made to the *grand chef*. Now she knew both the senior NCO, that drunken bull upstairs, the ship's captain and leading engineer were absent from the dry dock. Now there would be only that rabble of workmen, whose main concern seemed to get their greasy paws under the skirts of any woman they could find, and a bunch of raw boys still wet behind the ears. If the *grand chef* was going to pull it off at all, it was now or never.

She frowned at Simone who had serviced the bull upstairs. She was a fat girl with a vacant moon face, who looked like two sacks of potatoes tied together by the belt of her dressing gown that disappeared into the soft pillow of her massive stomach. 'Are you sure, he's out?' she asked in French urgently, knowing that the two *bodies* couldn't understand her native language.

Simone nodded and her double chin wobbled.

157

'*Bon*,' Madame Liz said. 'So they'll be able to take care of him without difficulty.' She looked out of the window hung with the usual red curtains. Out to sea a storm was brewing up. The spring sunshine had vanished. In its place there hung low, grey ominous clouds. Lightning flashed silently across the horizon, a sinister scarlet.

'What about these two pricks, Madame?' asked Janine, pretty, gamine, her black hair cropped like a schoolgirl's. She smiled sweetly at the two young U-boat men. 'Might as well get rid of them as well. Two less of the pricks.'

Madame Liz thought for a moment. She didn't like her place being used for this sort of thing, she didn't like it one bit. But she had been compromised by four years of occupation, and after the war, or after the arrival of the English, whichever took place first, she wanted no trouble with the authorities. A woman had to live, after all. So, like it or not, she had to do whatever the *grand chef* ordered. 'Yes,' she said finally, 'there's got to be no witnesses. They might as well go, too.' She smiled at the boys as well, who smiled back in a red-faced embarrassed manner, not realizing that at this moment their fate had just been decided.

Janine put her arm around the nearest sailor, stuck her tongue into his ear with professional concupiscence, breathing hard with faked passion. 'You wanna jig-jig?' she sighed in broken German, while, opposite, Simone opened her flowered dressing gown. Her massive breasts, the nipples a deep scarlet, dropped out automatically. 'Here, sailor-boy,' she proffered them to the open-mouthed U-boat man, 'have a suck of these!'

The boy flushed a brilliant red. 'The *Obermaat* said we wasn't to,' he stuttered, eyes wide open with awe at those tremendous dugs. 'Yer supposed to have a yellow card from the doctor, he sez —'

'Piss on the yellow card,' Simone growled and, grabbing the sailor by his cropped head, she pulled him towards her, muffling his protests in that mountain of white flesh.

Madame Liz shook her head, as Simone said in a bored sort of way, the boy's head firmly clutched to her bosom, 'Some of these *boches* are so dumb, they can't even eat soup with a frigging spoon...'

Christian and the LE plodded stolidly up the steep road that led to the dock, the wind whipping their uniforms about them tightly. Out to sea it was lashing the green water into a white fury. Thunder rumbled in the distance and over the horizon the lightning flashed, ripping the clouds apart in scarlet fury. 'Force eight,' Christian yelled above the wind. 'We're in for a right old damned squall!'

The LE nodded and pulled up his collar as the first drops of rain came pattering down, exploding in wet bursts on the cobbles. 'If I could only have got laid, it wouldn't matter —'

He stopped abruptly in mid-step, what looked like a large scarlet raindrop suddenly appearing on his chest, just above the Iron Cross. Christian stopped, too. The LE looked as if he were drunk. His eyes were rolling foolishly and his knees appeared to be buckled under him, mouth gaping absurdly. 'What's the matter, LE?' he demanded as the thunder echoed and re-echoed around the circle of the surrounding hills. 'Are you sick or —'

Startlingly, without any warning, the LE pitched straight forward onto the black gleaming cobbles of the *pavé*, his cap rolling off, the raindrops beginning to beat on his head.

'My God,' Christian breathed, as slow *tac-tac* noises came ever closer, 'he ... *he's dead...*!' Next moment he saw the angry little spurts of flame running rapidly towards him and he was throwing himself into a ditch, frantically tugging out his pistol, already knowing instinctively that the damned French Resistance was attacking…

The boy's scream had cut into Frenssen's dream like a sharp knife. In a flash he was out of the big bed, pistol in hand, boots in the other and onto the landing. Down below the men in the rough clothing of fishermen or the like were slaughtering the boy, slashing at his exposed neck with their knives, while others held him by the head as if they were gutting fish.

'*The boche!*' Madame Liz screamed, seeing him standing there at the head of the stairs, stark naked and staring down at the scene like an enraged bull.

One of the killers raised a pistol. Frenssen was quicker. He didn't even fire. Instead he flung his boot savagely. The Frenchman went reeling back, blood jetting from his nose, red nail-marks flashing across his pale face suddenly, as if someone had just walked over it.

Frenssen didn't wait for the rest to react. He dived down the stairs and smashed into the men holding the unfortunate sailor. His pistol flashed right and left. The man who had been slashing the sailor's throat howled with pain and fell to his knees spitting out bright teeth through red gore. 'Kid!' Frenssen yelled urgently. But the 'kid' was already dead or dying.

The bullet slammed into the wall just above Frenssen's head. The girls screamed. The men cried in anger. Frenssen grabbed hold of Madame Liz by her bun and propelled her in front of him, crying, 'And this ain't my salami sticking into her arse!'

One of the attackers raised his pistol to fire, but a terrified Madame Liz cried piteously to him, face contorted with fear. He lowered the gun.

Frenssen backed towards the door, wincing with pain on the broken glass. Out of the corner of his eyes he saw the other U-boat man. His flies were open and there was an ugly red gaping hole where his sexual organ had been. Frenssen cursed, sick at heart and nauseated. He had been the cause of the poor kids' deaths, just to get a little bit of shitting tail! The door opened. He could feel the first drops of cold rain on his naked back. He drew a great breath. Next moment he shoved Madame Liz forward straight at the Frenchman advancing on him. In an instant he had slammed the door to and was running for his life through the pouring rain, bullets cutting the air all around him…

Christian could see what had happened quite clearly now. The Resistance men had sneaked up on the workers along the jetty, using the big concrete wall as cover. It had probably taken them only seconds to start up the old-fashioned English Vickers machine gun and begin systematically wiping the workers out. Now the whole length of the dry-dock was littered with their still bodies, while on the far side of the submarine, a handful of the guard still held out, firing short bursts of Schmeisser fire at their attackers. As for the rest of the crew, he guessed from the firing from the direction of the huts on the other side of the water that the Resistance had them pinned down there. It was obvious what the French were after. They wanted to destroy Century One and flee before the main garrison over at Brest was alerted. But first they had to eradicate the few guards at the other end of that jetty. He screwed up his eyes and tried to count the numbers of the attackers, but gave up after he had reached fifty. The guards were outnumbered at least ten to one, and it wouldn't be long before the Frenchmen rushed them under the cover of that damned ancient machine gun which the English had probably dropped to them by parachute.

The sound of running feet alerted him to his danger here in the ditch. Of course, there were others of the Resistance lurking around outside the dock. Hadn't they shot poor old Carlsen and nearly shot him? He swung round, pistol gripped in a white-knuckled hand, and gasped with shock.

Frenssen, stark-naked, was galloping down the glistening road, body streaming with rain and actually steaming, arms going like pistons. 'Oh, my sainted aunt!' Christian gasped and then called carefully over the roll of the thunder and hiss of the rain, 'Frenssen, over here!'

The big *Obermaat* stopped, chest heaving. Near to him on the opposite side of the road to Christian, a dark angry face under a soaked beret popped up, rifle raised. Frenssen acted, even before Christian could shout a warning. The automatic in his hand barked. The Frenchman flew back, what looked like a red button planted firmly in the centre of his forehead. Frenssen ran and slid to the bottom of Christian's ditch in a flurry of mud.

'What...?' Christian began, then decided it was not worth pursuing the subject of why Frenssen had come running down the road as naked as the day he was born. Besides, he thought he knew the answer. Instead he snapped, 'That's the key to their whole attack — the machine gun.'

'Agreed, sir. Nobble that and the steam'd go out of their attack. Look, they're getting ready to rush 'em, our poor sods, now!'

Christian squinted against the pouring rain. Now the French had finished slaughtering the dockies. They were concentrating their fire against the tin hut which housed the guard, the bullets from the Vickers ripping the length of the place, striking up

162

lines of vicious red, making a hellish racket. Meanwhile another group of Frenchmen, weapons gripped in wet hands, were sneaking along the jetty, crouched well down. 'Once they get within rushing distance and into that dead ground to left of the hut at ten o'clock they'll rush our people,' he said, 'And after that, it's Century One.'

Frenssen nodded his big head, the raindrops streaming down his angry red face, 'And I'm not having it, either,' he growled dangerously.

At another time, Christian would have laughed out loud at the big noncom's anger, as if this attack were a personal affront — and perhaps it was; hadn't it forced him out of some whore's bed, while he was engaged in one of his famed 'mattress polkas'? But not now. The situation was too desperate. Instead he said, 'Are you with me, Frenssen?'

'The Vickers?'

'Yes.'

'What are we waiting for, sir?' Frenssen growled, wiping the raindrops off his face with his big paw. 'I'm just in the right mood to stick that frigging gun up some frog's skinny arse, that I am!'

And so with that terrible threat, the two of them started to crawl along the muddy ditch in the pouring rain, the rattle of small-arms fire getting ever louder.

CHAPTER 8

'Well, gentlemen, this is it!' General Barton, the commander of the US Fourth Infantry Division, announced a little ponderously, as befitted such a big, heavy man, and not without a sense of drama. 'The *last* exercise!'

There was a mutter and murmur of excitement, surprise, perhaps even fear from the assembled regimental and battalion commanders who one day would lead the great assault on Hitler's Europe.

Tubby Barton held up his hand for silence and the command was obeyed immediately. For a moment nothing was to be heard save the steady tread of the sentry on the gravel outside the briefing hut.

'According to the met, boys, on April 28th, the sea will be calm, a force three or four wind blowing, and the moon will be in its quarter. All in all, ideal conditions for a large-scale exercise at Slapton by ourselves and our friends of the First Engineer Special Brigade.' He nodded to the tall serious colonel who led the combat engineers.

At the back of the room, Savage, sitting with the other battalion commanders, frowned a little. How many times now had he sat in invasion planning committees, committees on North Africa, Sicily, Italy, and always it had seemed so easy at the committee stage. Invariably it had always ended in murder, mayhem, mass confusion, with that stupid stretch of beach, African, Sicilian, Italian, being bought at the cost of many young men's lives. He thought of Bloody Anzio and shuddered slightly. Hastily he dismissed the thought of that bloody massacre, and listened to what the big general had to say.

'The plan is as follows, gentlemen,' Tubby continued. 'Convoy C-4, that is the English Royal Navy's code-name for it, consisting of HMS *Azalea*, a corvette, whatever that is, and the destroyer HMS *Scimitar* as escorts, will leave Plymouth after dark on the 28th. The convoy will then sail eastwards,' he rapped the map of the south coast pinned on the blackboard next to him on the dais, 'here past Dartmouth and into Lyme Bay. Just before Portland Bill — here —' he rapped the map again — 'the convoy will swing round and the exercise will commence. The eight tank-landing craft will start discharging their cargoes, while your engineers, Colonel,' he nodded to the officer in charge of the First Engineer Special Brigade, 'will hit the beaches together with Colonel Savage's First Battalion. I don't have to tell you what your mission is there, you've all done it often enough before.' Tubby Barton forced a grin. 'But remember, this is the very last time and I want it to be done perfectly. Ike's eyes will be on you.' His grin disappeared. 'More importantly, the next time you'll do it, any mistakes will be paid for *in blood*! The next time it will be for real!'

The Commander of the Fourth Infantry Division paused to let his words sink in and all around him Savage could feel the mood changing as his fellows, none of them veterans like himself, realized the full implication of those words — *for real*.

'Now,' Barton went on, 'the weather, as I have said, is going to be as good as it ever will be, the troops are trained so well that they are becoming stale, and those English Royal Navy boys in the convoy have been doing this sort of thing ever since Dunkirk in '40 when a lot of you gentlemen weren't even in the Army. So, gentlemen, what can go wrong?' He grinned again and answered his own question, a little malicious twinkle in his eyes,' probably every damned thing — *and then some*!'

Savage shared the grin. He was beginning to like Tubby Barton; he was a soldier's soldier.

'Just as it will probably go wrong on the day and when it does, gentlemen, don't panic. Wrong or right, we are still going to win, you can bet your bottom dollar on that! *The US Army simply doesn't lose wars.*' There was iron in the big general's voice now. 'So having said that, let's roll up our sleeves and get down to cases. Now, number one, the question of security for you guys who are Bigots and who are going along on this exercise...' It was just then that Savage cast a glance through the window, the cold raindrops streaming down the panes like sad tears. Peewee was standing there. There was no mistaking the cocky little Texan bastard, the .45 slung low on his skinny hip, its leather thongs wrapped around the kid's thighs so that he looked like an old style gunslinger in his native state. And over these last weeks and months Peewee had developed a furtive, sly air, a knowing look on his freckled, cocky face, as if he knew more than he was telling, something which made him a man apart. Suddenly Savage visualized him when he was alone, practising draws with that big .45 in front of a mirror, legs spread, face set in a deliberate mean, tough way, whipping out the pistol and blasting off at himself in the glass. He shuddered and took his eyes away from the window swiftly...

Half an hour later, when they all emerged from the briefing hut into the thin cold drizzle, chatting excitedly to one another, self-important staff officers striding off to the waiting olive-drab Packards, briefcases obviously full of secrets tucked under their arms, Peewee was gone. But out beyond the divisional headquarters building, he could hear someone singing in an ugly plaintive drawl, '*The stars at night, are big and bright, Deep in the heart of Texas*' and he knew instinctively it was Peewee. That wasn't all. Out from over the green swaying Channel, he could hear the distant rumble of gunfire, ominous and threatening, as if the Krauts over there already knew they were coming and were demonstrating for the benefit of the conference just what was waiting for them on the 'day.'

Savage frowned and, tucking his head down against the rain, strode off through the mud, pursued by that silly jingle … *'Deep in the heart of Texas…'*

Christian wiped the raindrops from his furrowed forehead with the hand that held the pistol and hissed, 'We've got to wait till they change the belt. Probably take them about thirty … perhaps forty seconds … and then we've got to nobble them. Remember,' he peered through the grey rain-fog at the gunners, only fifty metres away now, and frowned, 'this'll be our own last chance. Muff it and that's the end of Century One.' He didn't add what he was thinking, though. It would mean the end of the crew, too.

'I'll nobble the fuckers all right!' Frenssen said grimly. 'Though I wish to all hell I had something to cover my, er, private parts with. It don't seem right to be going into the attack, with yer bits and pieces dangling for all to see, even if they are frogs.'

'I'd lend you my handkerchief, you big rogue,' Christian said and grinned, though he had never felt less like grinning, looking down at the giant's mud-stained loins, 'but somehow or other I don't think it'd do the job. It's a bit too small.'

'I've allus been told by the ladies that I was quite well built,' Frenssen said modestly. 'Look, sir, they're changing the belt!'

Christian wasted no more time. 'All right, Frenssen, *here we go!*'

Suddenly they were up on their feet, sliding a little in the mud as they breasted the ditch and doubled through the pelting rain to where the Frenchmen fumbled with the long gleaming belt of bullets. Skidding like a naked kangaroo, Frenssen lashed out with his foot at a Frenchman who poppedout of a hole to his front. The blow lifted him clean out of the hole and sent him flying, blood squirting in a thick stream from a smashed nose.

Another Frenchman yelled and swung round, rifle raised to face the two of them. 'Naughty, naughty!' Frenssen growled, carried away by the terrible excitement of combat. He fired — and missed hopelessly.

The Frenchman raised his rifle, a look of triumph in his dark eyes beneath the soaked beret.

Christian fired first. A huge hole appeared as if by magic in the Frenchman's chest, splintered white bone flecking the gory red mess, the pale grey of the viscera pulsating obscenely. They rushed on.

Now the Frenchmen manning the Vickers saw them. Frantically, the rain streaming down their crazed faces, they swung it round. Christian tensed. They were too late! The frogs had already fitted the new belt of ammo. He waited. There was no hope for them now. He could see the gunner's knuckles whiten as he pressed the twin handles, thumb on the trigger.

'*Look out*!' Frenssen screamed in an ecstasy of fear.

Nothing happened!

Christian didn't know whether to laugh or cry. 'Buckets of flying crap!' he cried wildly, knowing that he had been reprieved yet once again. '*They've got a stoppage!*'

'Oh, fucking hell, wonders never cease, *a stoppage*!' Frenssen hurtled forward, followed by Christian. An instant later they were swaying back and forth, slugging it out with the terrified gun-crew, while from the hut which housed what was left of the guard, a cry of encouragement rose as the sailors broke from their hiding place, firing from the hip as they charged straight into the demoralized Resistance men.

Christian slammed the butt of his useless pistol into the Frenchman's chin, telling himself breathlessly, his heart thumping madly, as if it might well burst out of his ribcage at any moment, they had done it. They had pulled off a miracle.

Century One was saved. *They could still carry out their vital mission, on which the fate of the 'One Thousand Year Reich' now depended…*

And across the narrow strip of sea, which separated the two young men whose fates were now inextricably linked, Colonel Savage paused at the little wicket gate to the house in which the Englishwoman lived (somehow he could never think of her as May). It had stopped raining and the sea had calmed down. Somewhere a leaking drainpipe was dripping. Otherwise there was no sound save for the mournful cries of the gulls. Carefully he looked to left and right but there was no sign of him, not even that damned jingle of his. He nodded and opened the gate, bottle clutched firmly in his big, capable hands.

She was on her knees on a little rubber mat, digging at the damp earth, a large straw basket full of plants next to her, so engrossed in her task that she did not even hear the squeak of the rusty gate.

Suddenly she looked up, trowel in hand and he said, 'Christ, May, you look like Greer Garson playing *Mrs Minniver*, I swear you do!'

She smiled in surprise. 'Perhaps all English women look like she does ... though not so pretty, of course,' she added hastily, as if she thought she was being too immodest. Abruptly she saw the bottle cradled in his hands. 'It's not Saturday, you know,' she said.

'Sure,' he answered easily.

'Then why?' She indicated the black market scotch.

'Why? Because I won't be here next Saturday.'

Her bottom lip trembled and for the first time since he had known her he thought, in dismay, that she was going to cry. 'You're going?' she gasped, her hand flying to her mouth. 'It's on, Sam ... the other thing?'

He shook his head slowly, staring at her, wondering how she could have become so concerned about him in such a short time, realizing that she was the only person left in the whole goddam world who cared whether he 'bought the farm' or not. 'No, May,' he reassured her. 'Just going this one Saturday. The other thing,' that was what they always called the Invasion, which both of them knew instinctively would separate them for good, 'is not on *just yet*. Just an exercise, pure and simple, May.'

She breathed an audible sigh of relief and said roguishly, 'Listen who's talking about *pure and simple* - with his Saturday night treat under his arm!'

'What a funny place to put it!' He played up to her game.

She shed her gloves. 'A tall glass is called for, I suppose?' She rolled her eyes.

'Why not two?'

'Could you stand it after a hard day at the office?' She fluttered her eyelids in mock modesty. 'You know what strong drinks do to us simple country maidens in bed, kind sir.'

Laughing arm in arm they passed into the dark Victorian house on the cliff, the wall above the elaborately carved door marked by the hole from the shell which had gone astray during an attack by the 'invaders' the previous year. It would be there long, long after they had disappeared into the footnotes of the history of World War Two...

CHAPTER 9

Christian took one last look through the periscope and barked almost savagely, 'Down tube!'

Smoothly, silently, the periscope slid back into the green fetid atmosphere of Century One, while the young crew waited.

Christian took his time while above him the Allied ships ploughed through the green Atlantic heading unwittingly towards their fate. 'Comrades,' Christian said, knowing that even those at their machines with their backs to him were hanging on to his every word, 'regard this as a demonstration of the power of Century One. We shall fire three fish *blind* - and hit our target each time. Comrades, we are sailing in a revolutionary boat and using revolutionary weapons.'

He caught Frenssen's look and knew what the big *Obermaat* was thinking. Why after all the fuss and bother with Century One, had they now sailed into the Atlantic on what seemed an ordinary combat patrol? What could be so decisive and war-winning about sinking enemy freighters, however big? Christian ignored the look. His greenbeaks had to be encouraged, given an easy victory, before their real mission commenced.

'Trim perfect, *Oberleutnant* von Cheetham,' his new LE barked.

Again Christian wondered at that strange name, although the tall blond young Prussian had explained almost as soon as he had come aboard; 'Scottish mercenaries, sir. Fled Scotland for Prussia, strictly from hunger back in the 18th century; ennobled by Frederick the Great for knocking the heads off sundry Polacks, Frogs and Austrians!' Now, however, he concentrated on the demonstration.

'Open fire,' he ordered the torpedo officer quite calmly.

The excited young sub-lieutenant yelled; '*Fire … fire … fire!*'

'Hard left rudder … steer two fifty!' Christian commanded.

Suddenly the boat tensed. A slight shudder, another, and another. Von Cheetham glanced hastily at the trim, as the two-ton torpedoes slid into the water.

Christian began to count off the seconds as the deadly acoustic torpedoes swarmed out to find their targets, a nerve ticking electrically at his temple. A sudden shudder. A muffled roar. Century One lurched dramatically. Frenssen grabbed hold of a stanchion hastily. Von Cheetham swallowed hard. Christian tried to remain calm. 'One down … two to go…' he began as the boat trembled again. 'Correction,' he said, voice not quite steady, affected as always by the thrill of the chase, '*two* down and *one* to go!'

Frenssen wiped the sweat off his brick-red face and sniffed hard, for he was still suffering from a dreadful cold after that soaking in the pouring rain. 'Taking its frigging time, ain't it —'

The Century One heeled violently and von Cheetham cried, 'Holy Strawsack, that must have been a shitting big one!'

Christian sprang into action. 'Up periscope!' he rasped. Hastily he pushed his battered white cap round so that the tarnished peak was at the back of his head, then bent to receive the shining steel tube. Hurriedly he swung it round, as the green mist started to reveal the heaving waves. '*Wonderful!*' he breathed as the freighter came into view, listing to port, thick black smoke pouring out of her right up to the sullen grey sky. 'Seven thousand-ton freighter!' he
cried. Someone cheered. Frenssen frowned. Christian swung the circle of calibrated glass round further, turning on high

power for better vision. A tanker slid into the circle, a great blowtorch of flame searing her long deck, tiny black figures already throwing themselves off her bow in wild panic. 'Tanker,' he called to the crew, 'perhaps a ten thousand-tonner!' He flung the periscope another thirty degrees further and stopped abruptly. 'Cargo ship, perhaps five thousand tons, out of control,' he reported, as the enemy ship turned in slow circles, her rudder jammed, but no smoke or flame emerging from her as with the other two.

Behind him von Cheetham whistled softly. 'My God,' he said, voice awed, 'twenty-two thousand tons with three fish, all fired blind!'

Suddenly the crew was cheering wildly and Christian knew he had them. The greenbeaks thought they were veterans already. But there was one more thing to show them, he knew. 'Take her up, LE,' he commanded, voice suddenly very bleak. 'And gun crew stand by!'

Minutes later the U-boat heaved out of the water, perhaps six hundred metres away from the three stricken ships she had torpedoed, and the gun crew was running heavily in their nailed boots along the dripping, heaving deck towards the 88mm cannon.

Vainly the crippled cargo ship tried to engage the submarine with her own gun. A shell screamed from it and dropped well short of the U-boat, sending up a fountain of wild, white water. Another dropped beyond the Century One.

'Trying to frigging bracket us!' Frenssen yelled and cried to his gun crew, 'Well don't just stand there like a wet fart waiting to hit the side of the thunderbox — *FIRE*!'

The tremendous 88mm shell screeched across the intervening distance. It slammed into the side of the cargo ship with a great hollow boom. It reeled crazily, its superstructure almost touching the waves, and that was that; its crew started to take to the boats in wild panic, men even throwing themselves into the icy sea in their terror.

Christian watched stonily, as the three vessels, spewing black clouds of smoke, flecked here and there a bright cherry-red, began to go to their doom. 'LE,' he commanded, 'bring the crew up in batches. I want them to see this. It is not a question of how many tons of shipping we sink, but one of good ships … *and men*, men like ourselves!'

'Sorry, sir,' von Cheetham answered, chastened, and began to bring up the crew as the U-boat steered ever closer to the survivors; some in boats; others already dead, slopping up and down in the valleys of escaping oil like black glistening logs; and many waving frantically, trying to escape before that nauseating, cloying oil swamped them for good.

Christian remembered the ill-fated U-82 and those terrible three days on the raft, alone in the vast burning sweep of the Indian Ocean, and commanded a horrified von Cheetham, 'You speak, English, LE. Tell them we can't take them aboard. But we'll radio their position in clear immediately. Tell them to group together. They'll have a better chance of being rescued that way. Tell them — good luck.' He turned away, unable to bear the sight of those pathetic creatures, who were his fellow men, lurching up and down in the dark mysterious valleys of the killing diesel oil. Around him he could hear the greenbeaks talking, voices muted now, all excitement vanished, as they surveyed their victims. He frowned and told himself they were learning … they were learning all right.

'*Alarrmmm…*' the lookout yelled frantically, as the seaplane materialized from the west as if by magic. '*Aircraft from the sun… ALARM!*'

Christian hit the panic button. The sirens shrilled. The deck crew came sliding down the ladder, shedding water everywhere. The hatch clanged shut in the same instant that the first depth charges began exploding all around them, sending the U-boat reeling from one side to the other, as if punched savagely back and forth by a great steel fist.

Century One surfaced involuntarily, then crash-dived almost the next moment, going straight down at a crazy angle. Depth charges burst all around. They ducked under those tremendous blows, the greenbeaks' faces ashen with shock and fear.

Century One shook time and time again with the impact. Rivets burst like taut string. Bolts cracked. Water seeped in through cracks in her hull everywhere. Grimly Christian took her down and down, knowing instinctively that they were going to pay now for their easy victory two hours before. The Tommies had spotted the Century and they were out for blood.

'Stop engines,' he commanded. 'Silent running.'

'Silent running,' von Cheetham echoed, his young face pale and glazed as if with Vaseline.

Now they waited in silence, each man wrapped up in a cocoon of his own thoughts, as the enemy seaplanes dived and the destroyers swept back and forth, launching their deadly black eggs. Below they shivered and sweated as the ocean rumbled and roared, tossing the boat back and forth under the impact of those ferocious explosions.

Time passed. The biting acrid fumes began to escape from their batteries. Men choked, eyes bulging from their sockets like those of the demented. Hastily Christian had the potash masks passed out, but they did not help much and here and there he could see his young sailors nodding off, falling into that final sleep from which there was no awaking; and all the time Frenssen eyed him sullenly, almost angrily, as if to say; why are you subjecting them to this torture?

At three that afternoon Christian knew he must put an end to this purgatory, cost what it may. His young men couldn't stand much more. All around him they were drawing half-clean, hot air through the potash masks, coughing and choking all the time as if they were advanced cases of TB.

'Take her up, LE,' he commanded quietly. 'We'll chance using the snort.'

Von Cheetham nodded, face crimson with the lack of oxygen, and began to ease the boat upwards, the noise of the depth charges seeming to be further away now. But Christian was not grabbing at straws, false hopes. He knew from bitter experience just how persistent the Tommies were. What was it the Big Lion always said about his bitter enemies; 'The German has a heavy voice and a soft hand, but the English, they have a soft voice and a *very heavy hand!*'

Metre by metre they rose, with the LE keeping an anxious eye on the trim before he announced softly, as if the enemy up top might well hear, 'We can use the snort now, sir.'

'Use snort!' he commanded and felt his ears pop suddenly. He knew immediately what had happened. A vacuum had occurred because the float of the *Schnorchel* had jammed in the closed position. 'Quick, take her down again,' he yelled, security thrown to the winds, as the crew who had put down their masks in anticipation of real fresh air began to gasp frantically, eyes bulging.

But even with the *Schnorchel* head below the surface, the valve remained jammed. Breathing became impossible. Suffocation was imminent. The men ripped at their singlets and collars in an attempt to get more air. But there was none.

The LE gesticulated wildly. He wanted the writhing sweating sailors to lay down the air mast. Only a few answered his call. They were, for the most part, concerned with their own fate, knowing — even the greenest of them — that they were dying already.

Frenssen staggered forward like a drunk. With agonizing slowness, aided by the LE and Christian, they lowered the life-giving mast, and somehow erected it again. Now men were lying on the deck among the dirty sea water, gasping out their last breaths. They were dying — *visibly* — before Christian's eyes. He prayed it would work.

Suddenly sea water came pouring down the air mast in a cold fury. They choked on. There was an abrupt obscene plop like a giant breaking wind, and in an instant clean sea air was sucked into the boat with a long passionate sigh at the same moment that the English destroyers gave up their search and began to turn for home.

Lying on a steel bench, his face contorted with pain as his eardrums threatened to explode at any moment, swallowing frantically to equalize the pressure, Christian sagged and told himself they had been saved for the great mission yet once again…

'So there goes Ireland,' Frenssen said, as the light of Fastnet Rock, near the southernmost tip of neutral Ireland, disappeared into the gloom and the revolutionary new submarine began to head for Lizard Head, the southwestern spur of England. 'It is the English Channel after all, sir. I thought it would be all along … and it's not the Invasion either, sir, is it?'

Christian sniffed, enjoying the cool night air in the conning tower, and said nothing.

But the two of them, the big petty officer with his burly, savagely muscled shoulders, and the harshly handsome slim young officer, had been together for too long for them to be able to keep secrets from one another. They were like an old married couple who could read each other's thoughts long before they were ever expressed. Frenssen said; 'Don't you think you'd better tell them now what it's all about, sir? They didn't do too badly — for wet-tails — during the attack.' He tried to toss the dewdrop off the end of his red nose with a swing of his head, but failed; the wind was too strong. 'Might as well get it over and done with, sir. If they're gonna cream their shivvies, let 'em do it now.'

Christian broke his heavy silence, listening to the throb of the diesels as they began to take the boat through the calmer coastal waters. 'You have a way of expressing yourself, you big rogue. You must have been brought up on Goethe's works.'

'*Goethe*!' Frenssen whipped away the offending moisture with his thumb and forefinger. 'Is he the bloke who writes that hot dirty-book stuff?'

Christian sighed and made his decision. 'All right, Frenssen, I suppose you're right. They ought to know what they're in for.'

'Not a combat patrol in the English Channel, sir?' Frenssen gasped. 'By the Great Whore of Buxtehude, kill a Tommy in these waters and all hell is let loose. Two boats a day were buying it here in the Channel before Big Lion called off our last offensive in '40 —'

'Not a combat patrol.' Christian cut off the excited flow of words. 'Something else, something very special.' He felt renewed confidence surge through his weary, jaded body as he remembered that secret conference back in Brest. 'Something very much more important than that.'

'So the Atlantic cruise was simply —'

'Training, Frenssen, training. An opportunity for the crew to settle down in the quickest possible way — under combat conditions.'

Frenssen nodded his big head. 'I understand, sir. So what is this great, top-secret action of ours?'

By way of an answer Christian said, 'Go down to my cabin. There is no sauce for you to steal there, so I feel quite safe in letting you loose. Underneath my bunk you'll find two steel helmets —'

'*Steel frigging helmets!*'

Christian ignored the protest and said, 'Take them out and bring them to the control room. I need them to brief the crew. Now be off with you.'

Muttering to himself, Frenssen clattered down the dripping ladder to carry out the skipper's orders, leaving Christian to stare thoughtfully at the dark smudge on the horizon which was England. Then, almost as an afterthought, he looked at the green-glowing dial of his issue chronometer. It was exactly midnight on the morning of Saturday 28th April 1944.

CHAPTER 10

Like beasts of burden, laden with equipment and weapons, each soldier's helmet bearing a chalked number, the men of the First Battalion filed down the centuries' old steps to the waiting barges.

Out to sea the sun had disappeared, but it still lit the shattered seaport a rosy hue, hiding the scars of the years of bombing that Plymouth had suffered since 1939. The gulls wheeled and cried, diving low over the departing boats, as if they were expecting the same offerings the fishermen had once given them. But they were to be disappointed. Some of the GIs waiting to be taken out to the big transports were already being seasick miserably; that was the only offering the gulls were to receive this April day.

Savage watched with a practised eye, noting that his platoons were filing forward correctly to land in reverse order, with the assault teams, heavily laden with bazookas, machine guns and flame throwers, hitting the beaches first. All was going well, perhaps too well. But then again, he reminded himself, this wasn't going to be another bloody Anzio; this was only a practice exercise.

He turned his attention to the bay where the convoy was beginning to form up, the two escorts from the Royal Navy already making steam and shrilling their sirens, while the big five thousand-ton transports wallowed in the swell, waiting for their human cargoes. The tanks and the DUKWs, which would carry the assault infantry, were already loaded; twenty-odd tanks to each ship and four DUKWs, known invariably to the GIs as 'ducks' or even 'frigging ruptured ducks!'

'Sir,' a polite New England voice broke into his thoughts.

He turned. It was one of the umpires, a young captain with steel GI glasses. 'Yes?'

'You can board now, sir. They're going to embark your battalion.' The captain hesitated, as Savage stepped forward.

'What is it?' the latter asked.

The young captain looked embarrassed. 'It's your — er — bodyguard, sir,' he answered hurriedly, putting his thin hand up to his mouth as old woman do when they are about to cough, as if they are afraid their false teeth might slide out.

'You mean Peewee —' Savage began.

'Here I am, Colonel, sir. No sweat, sir. Just taking a piss before we boarded.'

Savage turned and frowned. It was Peewee all right, helmet tilted rakishly to one side, unlit stub of a cigar stuck in the corner of his mouth and that damned gun slung from his hip. He looked even more like a 19th century bad man à la Hollywood. 'Okay, *Wyatt Earp*, get on board the boat!' he snapped, as the captain saluted and went on his way.

For a moment he turned and stared at bombed-out Plymouth, as out in the bay the whistles shrilled and the hooters sounded their dire warning.

Back in November '42, Mary-Lou had cried in Washington as he had kissed her for the last time, and at Newport, Virginia, just before they had embarked for Operation Torch, he had turned and saluted the shore, saluted America, in a young man's oddly dramatic gesture, as if he had thought he would never see it again. Now, slowly, he raised his hand to his helmet, bearing the silver insignia of a colonel on it, and saluted once more. '*Remember, we're the class of '42, Sam,*' she had said almost happily, and she hadn't cried like Mary-Lou. '*What can happen to old hands like us?*' All the same, he saluted the shattered city as if it was important to do so. Moments later he was gone, bobbing up and down on the rocking barge, Peewee watching him as if his very life depended on it...

Twenty miles away or so, Christian Jungblut waited till the men had had their first delighted drink of beer which he had ordered broken out for this special occasion, before he began. There, at two hundred feet below the English Channel, his open-faced greenbeaks eyed him expectantly, and *Obermaat* Frenssen, his can of beer emptied in one huge greedy draught, wondered if he could talk one of the wet-tails out of his before it was too late.

'Comrades,' he said finally, 'it is time that I tell you what our real mission is. I'm sorry that I have not been able to do so up to now...' He shrugged and left the sentence unfinished. 'However, our present mission is of the utmost importance, which if successful, might change the whole course of the war.'

Opposite him, Frenssen picked up *Oberleutnant* von Cheetham's beer (the LE's attention was concentrated exclusively on Christian) and drained it in one furtive gulp. He belched pleasurably.

Swiftly Christian began to explain to his greenbeaks the problems facing the Greater German General Staff in making their assessment of where the Anglo-Americans would land in France; how it had been discovered that there was a special kind of Anglo-American officer who knew where the landing beaches were; and how vital it was to discover that secret before it was too late to revise Field Marshal Rommel's defences along the Atlantic Wall. He explained, too, how these officers in the know were code-named 'Bigots', a reversal, so it was thought, of an earlier code-word used by the Western Allies for Operation Torch, their invasion of North Africa; '*To*

Gib, for Gibraltar — in 1942, our Intelligence people have worked out, that was the cover name for all top secret documents used in the operation. So when they planned the new Invasion they simply turned that "TOGIB" around and made it "BIGOT".'

Even Frenssen forgot the beer, now intrigued by Christian's explanation. All of them, even the most stupid, wondered where all this was leading. Christian, for his part, was amused a little by the irony of it all. Here they were, deep beneath the English Channel, the most dangerous stretch of water in the whole world for a German U-boat, discussing secret codes.

'Now,' he continued, 'this is what is soon to happen not far from here. An Allied convoy, protected by ships of the English Royal Navy, is about to sail from Plymouth, west of here. In that convoy will be some of the Ami soldiers who will carry out the real invasion one day soon.' He hesitated for only a fraction of a second. 'Among those soldiers will be a few, at least three Intelligence thinks, who are Bigots, *who know the great secret!* Just before dawn — presumably that will be the time when the Anglo-Americans will launch the real attack on France — the exercise these men are to carry out will commence. When that happens, Century One will be in position right underneath that convoy.'

Oberleutnant von Cheetham whistled softly. 'Are we going to attack it with the new acoustics, sir?' he asked quickly.

Christian shook his head. 'No, *not we*! The E-boat squadron from Cherbourg has been selected for that particular task. As soon as the convoy has been reported there, they will make a high-speed dash across the Channel under cover of darkness and attack the convoy. It is their job to torpedo one or more of the troop transports and *draw off*,' he emphasized the words carefully, 'the naval escorts so that we can do *our* job.'

He paused and, letting the words sink in, uncovered the two helmets which lay in front of him on the little metal flap.

The crew stared at the American helmets, both battered, one with a ragged hole in it as if it had been struck by a bullet, in wonder. What had they got to do with their mission, whatever it damn well might be? 'Make good pisspots!' Frenssen ventured, but no one laughed. They were all too tense.

Christian pointed his forefinger at the tarnished insignia on the two helmets. 'Mark well this silver star,' he said deliberately, 'and this silver American eagle. Mark the two *very* well. Everything depends on the ability of anyone who might carry out deck watch when the attack goes in recognizing them and informing me *immediately*. Look!' he commanded.

They looked, trying to imprint them on their mind's eye. Even Frenssen, his usual cynicism momentarily vanished, stared at the helmets as if his life depended upon it.

'Both those insignia,' Christian continued after a few moments, 'indicate that their wearer is a lieutenant or full colonel in the US Army, and, comrades, it is in that rank that we shall find our precious Bigots.'

'*We?*' von Cheetham queried sharply.

'Yes, *we*. When one or more of the transports have been torpedoed and — God willing — the E-boat chappies have drawn away the escorts, we surface.'

'*Whew!*' someone whistled sharply. 'Surfacing in the middle of the English Channel! That's gonna be hairy.'

'Very hairy indeed. But it's got to be done. For it will be our task to pick up a Bigot.' He licked his bottom lip, as if he were suddenly very dry. '*And remember, comrades, find that Bigot and we win the war on the beaches of France…* !'

The *LST 507* wallowed in the calm sea, chugging steadily eastwards at a five-knot speed. Grouped around her in the pale, spectral light of the quarter moon were the dim shapes of the other seven tank-landing ships, plunging and wallowing like clumsy whales; while the two escorts, white bones at their teeth, dashed in and out, chivvying and worrying them like sheep dogs, trying to keep the convoy up close.

Savage took his gaze off the escorts and said to his assembled officers, 'There is no real danger, according to Intelligence, gentlemen. But the Royal Navy is thorough and experienced in these things. They're trying to avoid getting any stragglers.'

'Quite right, too,' the tall bespectacled colonel of engineers butted in. For some reason he was carrying a slide-rule. Savage told himself perhaps he carried it as a Greek might carry his worry-beads. 'There are E-boats just over there at Cherbourg and the *Luftwaffe* is only twenty minutes' flying time away. They'd like nothing better than a big fat tub like this to attack. Wouldn't stand a chance at this speed.' He eased his helmet with the bright silver eagle on the front and Savage told himself the colonel of engineers was nervous; he had never been in combat before. But, then again, neither had his own officers.

'Let's not try to get nervous, Colonel,' he said easily. 'Radar has got us nice and tightly covered and if you're thinking of Kraut subs, forget it. There hasn't been one reported in the English Channel, I am reliably informed, for months, perhaps even years now. It's far too dangerous for them.'

'Yeah, I suppose you're right, Colonel,' the engineer agreed, fiddling with his slide-rule as if he wished he was back in his civilian practice, his only worry realtors trying to screw him out of a profit.

Savage turned back to his officers. 'Let's forget the Krauts,' he snapped, 'and concentrate on the mission. *One*; I want you to watch the guys going down the nets. If they get excited they become careless and fall. And I don't want any casualties in the Battalion. It's too late to train new men. *Two*; once we hit the beach, I want the two assault companies to go like hell for Slapton Mere. Ride 'em hard, and again — watch out for casualties. I don't want any more fatalities due to our own —'

He stopped short. Across the water there was a hollow boom and a sudden rending of torn metal. He strained his eyes in the silver gloom. One of the assault boats had come to a sudden stop. A siren started to shrill urgently.

'What is it, Colonel?' Major Hawkie, his Exec., asked, voice worried, 'Not E-boats!'

'*Nervous frigging nelly*!' Savage cursed to himself and focused his night glasses swiftly. Aloud, he said, 'Of course, not, Hawkie! Looks to me like a collision. The big tub seems to have … hit one of the English escorts.' Now he could see the Aldis lamp flicking off and on rapidly from the bridge of the corvette HMS *Azalea* and cursed inwardly that he could not read the signal. In war, the slower guy — the one who didn't get the message fast enough — bought the farm. 'Hey, Hawkie, get up to the bridge. My compliments to the skipper and all that naval kind of crap,' he snarled. 'Find out what the Sam Hill's going over there, toot-sweet!'

'Yessir!' Hawkie snapped and actually saluted before he doubled away to carry out Savage's order.

Five minutes later he was back. 'You were right, sir,' he explained. 'There has been a collision. HMS *Azalea* reports that the destroyer HMS *Scimitar* has hit one of the LSTs.'

'Shit!' Savage cursed bitterly. 'Does that frigging well mean the frigging exercise is cancelled?'

'Oh, my aching back,' one of his company commanders moaned. 'Not again. I couldn't stand one more exercise! I'd go ape, *plain goddam ape-shit.*'

'No sir,' Hawkie said hastily. 'The LST has suffered only superficial damage, apparently. But according to the *Azalea*, the *Scimitar* has been badly holed. She has been ordered back to Plymouth.'

Savage frowned. 'That means...' He didn't finish the sentence. He didn't need to. They all knew as well as he did what that meant. A couple of thousand GIs were now at sea, with nothing to defend them save one lone corvette; HMS *Azalea*. If the Krauts came they wouldn't have a chance...

CHAPTER 11

Their Lordships' signal was faint, but definite. The huge listening towers manned by the *Kriegsmarine's* de-coding service at Flensburg and Hamburg picked it up immediately. Below in their underground bunkers the bespectacled decoders, German products of America's Ivy League colleges and Britain's Oxbridge, went to work at once. They knew the code. They knew the situation. Within fifteen minutes flat the languid young men, with their affected air and handkerchieves tucked up their sleeves in the slightly decadent English manner, had de-coded it and sent it winging off on its way to the Big Lion's headquarters in Brest.

Dönitz didn't hesitate. There was not a minute to be lost. Within seconds he was on the red scrambler-phone to the E-boat flotilla at Cherbourg. The commodore there had hardly put the phone down when the sirens began to shriek their urgent warning the length of the dripping jetty. The pasty-faced young men in their leather overalls snapped into action at once. Here and there some of them ran up the *Kriegsmarine's* battle-flag, but most of the young men commanding the lean, lethal motor torpedo-boats hoisted their own very personal emblems; a pair of red flannel drawers taken from some French granny; a broom in two cases; and the usual silk frilly pants 'won' from the whores.

Otto, the flotilla's comedian, had to be different, of course.

As he pressed the button and the E-boat's tremendous motors burst into life, shaking the light wooden craft so that it seemed about to fall apart at any moment, he hoisted his own personal battle standard; a black brassiere *with three cups*!

Proudly he gazed at it, as the sirens shrilled and the motors raced, with excited seamen clattering up and down the jetty urgently. 'The sign of the three tits,' he announced to no one in particular. 'What better way is there to go to war?' He blew a wet kiss at the absurd bra and then yelled, iron in his harsh young voice, '*Leinen los*!' On the jetty the dockmen hurriedly cast off the stout ropes. 'Shut all watertight doors!' Otto commanded, as the boat trembled and vibrated like a thoroughbred greyhound impatient to be let off its lead. '*Los, dalli ... dalli...* Let go of your stern cable!'

A faint splash. The clatter of the nailed boots as the deckhands hurried to whip the wire rope aboard before it could fall and foul the screws.

'Let go your forrard!' Otto commanded. He waited just an instant, then called; 'Full power!'

The lead motorboat slid away immediately. On the bridge, Otto felt the boat kick as it hit the first wave. Automatically his stomach muscles tightened against the battering to come. All about him the rest of the flotilla was cutting the water, churning the sluggish green into a brilliant white froth. The noise of the motors rose ear-splittingly. They started to gather speed. Now they were out of the harbour. Otto eased the throttle forward even more. The engines howled. The other young skippers did the same. One by one their keen bows rose out of the sea. More speed. Twin white trails of wild spray flashed upwards. Now they were hitting the waves solidly at nearly forty knots an hour, going all out, heading due west for England.

All was dark now. But on the bridge of Otto's boat the glowing green dials illuminated his sharply handsome face, as his gaze darted keenly from left to right and back again; the hunter intent on his prey...

'Check that everyone is wearing his life-belt!' Savage ordered urgently, 'The Navy guys have spotted something on their radar.'

'Probably one of the other convoys, sir,' Hawkie said. 'There is one due to sail on a parallel course to ours, coming up from Land's End. Seven Allied Merchantmen heading for Portsmouth. The skipper of the *507* told me.'

'Probably,' Savage agreed, 'but check them all the same. You know how careless dough-faces are.'

'Wilco, sir!' Hawkie snapped and disappeared into the darkness, stopping at each faintly seen group of GIs to call, 'Got your life-belts, you guys…? Got your life-belts?'

Moodily Savage walked over to the rail and stared out at the dark rolling sea, little flashes of white indicating waves. How many nights had he spent like this, he wondered, staring out at the sea in crowded troop-ships, asking himself what the morrow would bring? He smiled a little wearily. It seemed like a whole goddam life-time, as if he had never known anything else but war and violence and sudden death. He spat over the side.

'How's it going, Colonel, sir?' It was Peewee. Nobody else in the Battalion dared call him 'Colonel, sir.'

He turned round slowly, controlling himself with difficulty, knowing that if he flared up like he wanted to the damned little Texan bastard would know he was scared. He sniffed, 'All right, Peewee,' he said in a non-committal fashion, staring down at the little Texan in his oversized helmet. 'How's it going with you?' At that moment he hated himself for being such a hypocrite. But the Texan was a jinx. He knew it, and instinctively he felt he couldn't afford to offend him.

'Oh, okay, Colonel, sir, I guess,' the other man said slowly, as if he weren't quite sure if everything *were* okay. 'I'll be kind of glad when all these here exercises are over and the real thing starts. Hell, you know what they say, Colonel, *war is hell, but peacetime kills ya!*' He laughed at his own joke softly.

Savage knew the little bastard was not boasting. He'd seen his kind before in the Third; lonely little men who thrived on war and violence, the guys who always volunteered for patrols and never admitted, like most of the doughs would, that they were scared of anything. No, Peewee really would *enjoy* combat. 'Well, it won't be long now, Peewee,' he said tonelessly, staring across at the dark outline of the *Azalea*, a little annoyed again because he could not read the white flickering of the Aldis lamp being worked on her bridge.

''Spect it won't, Colonel, sir.' Peewee slapped his pistol butt loudly and Savage started a little at the sudden noise. 'Been toting these pieces around for over two years now, sir. Wish to hell I could get me a chance to use this 'un *for real* at last!'

Savage grunted something, wishing he'd go away. In Peewee's presence he felt shivery and flushed, as if he had been hit by another attack of malaria.

Peewee grinned up at him in the darkness, 'Guess I'll go down below and see what those Navy guys have got over in the way of chow. This sea air sure makes a man hungry.' And with that he was gone, without a salute, casually, as if it was every day, Savage told himself angrily, that that goddam prick of a private first class talked to a colonel.

But he knew why the little Texan did it. Peewee had seen through him. He knew that Savage didn't want to die, that he feared him, knew that one day … one awful day… Angrily Savage spat over the side again and decided he wouldn't think that particularly unpleasant thought to its logical end, not this particular night anyway.

Christian felt comfortable and relatively safe for the first time since Century One had entered the English Channel. With the boat protected by fourteen metres of water and the blackness of the night above, radar detection of the snort's float and, his scope was almost impossible. He, too, had received Big Lion's message, giving the vital position and direction of Convoy C-4. He also knew something that the E-boat skippers already well on their way across the narrow strip of water between France and England didn't know, that the convoy was now guarded by one single Royal Navy ship. For some reason the other escort had turned back to port. Now, in essence, he told himself, it was a matter of the E-boats sinking one of the transports, scattering the unfortunate Ami stubble-hoppers into the water and luring away the escort so that he could surface and, with a bit of luck, pick up one of those Bigots.

At night it would be tricky, he knew that, but in the confusion, and secure in the knowledge that the RAF would not bomb him surrounded by their own people, he would risk using his searchlights to find the man — or men — they had come to capture.

'Sir,' one of the hydrophone operators cut into his thoughts, 'Sound band starboard ahead!' he reported briskly.

Christian tensed. This was it. It was the convoy. He passed to the periscope at once. About him the crew, dressed in their blue knitted underwear, working in their stockinged feet to keep down the noise, moved about their duties briskly, throwing covert glances at Christian all the time. 'Up scope,' he ordered softly. 'Right so.'

He bent and peered into the glass as it broke the surface. A spectral moon bathed the sea in an icy, hostile light. He swung it round towards the sound of the engines.

Suddenly they were there. Black mountains in perfect formation, seeming to fill the sky, totally unconcerned. But why should they be? They were in the safety of the English Channel, weren't they, with land in sight?

He swung the periscope the length of the convoy, his frown deepening by the instant as he took in the superstructures, the funnels, even the paintwork of the big, fat slow ships plodding steadily eastwards. Slowly, very slowly, he rose from the scope, while the crew watched him tensely. 'That's … that's not it,' he announced, voice flat and puzzled.

'What, sir?' von Cheetham asked.

'It's not the damned military convoy, man!' Christian snapped angrily. 'There's some mistake… *That's a bloody convoy of merchant ships up there!*'

'We who are about to die, salute thee, oh great tits!' Otto declared solemnly, saluting his stupid banner, as the convoy heaved into view two sea-miles away from where Christian now slumped bewildered and not a little angry.

To port, some five hundred metres away, Barthels, the flotilla commander, gave his craft full throttle. The E-boat's curved prow lifted out of the water at once. At forty knots an hour, it surged into the attack, hitting each wave with a solid, stomach-churning thud.

'*Full ahead!*' Otto yelled above the ear-splitting racket, as the E-boats raced towards the convoy.

Tracer, cold, hard and white, began to zip towards the big ships in a lethal morse. Somewhere a 40mm cannon started to chatter frantically. A flare exploded above the big slow ships. Barthels answered with a star shell which bathed the sea a glowing silver, throwing the enemy vessels into stark relief. A gun boomed on one of them and a great fountain of water erupted only metres away from Otto's boat, drenching the bridge. 'Perverted banana-suckers!' Otto cried happily, too carried away by the tremendous excitement of the hunt to be afraid. 'You'll pay for...' He stopped abruptly, mouth gasping open like a village idiot. '*Gott im Himmel!*' he gasped as he recognized the nearest ship, and then he was yelling frantically at his radio-man, 'Sparks... Sparks, urgent signal to the flotilla commander ... *we're attacking the wrong frigging convoy!*'

Savage watched the silent white lights on the horizon, flecked every now and again with a burst of vicious scarlet, and recognized them for what they were — a fire-fight. After all, he had seen them often enough.

'Some poor sucker's taking a beating,' a voice in the crowded darkness said in pity.

'Yeah,' another replied, 'the scuttlebutt is that we're running parallel with another convoy of merchantmen... Poor fuckers are under attack.'

'Better them than us,' a third.

'Yeah, you ain't shitting, buddy!' the first voice agreed enthusiastically.

'*You ought to have been a writer, Sam,*' she had said to him, 'a writer of novels. Then we could both have been your characters. I could have been your Mrs Minniver ... and you could have been the brave upstanding officer and gentleman.' He had realized even then that the unaccustomed scotch had made her a little drunk, but most of the time he had spent with women these last two years or so they had been a little drunk and desperate. So he had humoured her, asking gently, 'What do you mean, er, May?' He always hesitated over the name; perhaps it made her too real, too permanent; he preferred what he always called her in his own mind — 'the Englishwoman'.

'*What do you think I bloody well mean?*' she had retorted, a little flushed, a lock of blonde hair, dyed, hanging over her forehead. He had noted, too, that one of her breasts was working loose from the thin material of her nightdress. '*Don't you know? You've invented us, Sam Savage! I'm not Greer Garson in Mrs Minniver, all gentle and noble and lady of the bloody manor! I'm a desperate trollop!*' she had blurted out, and now he forgot that delightful left breast, seeing the tears suddenly flush her eyes.

'And me? How have I invented *me?*' he had asked. It was like combat fatigue. It was no use bottling it up, you had to get it off your chest or you'd be ruined — a coward — for the rest of your life.

'*You!*' She had flashed him a glance, a mixture of hate and love, '*You've cast yourself as...*' She had hesitated, bottom lip quivering, as if even at this moment of angry passion she could not bring herself to say the truth.

'Go on,' he urged gently.

'*You have damn well cast yourself in the role of the soldier who is bound to die!*'she had cried, the tears beginning to stream down her face now. '*But why? Only characters in cheap novels are condemned right from the start. Oh, Sam, there is a way out!*' She had hung her head, her naked shoulders racked with sobs, face buried in her hands so that he had hardly been able to hear her last words; '*You don't need to die ... do you?*'

'Holy cat!' an urgent voice yelled, 'Willya get a load of that?' He forgot the Englishwoman and flashed a look across the railing.

It was HMS *Azalea*. Suddenly she was heading out to sea at full speed, a white bone in her teeth, her sirens shrilling an urgent warning. He could just make out the tiny white figures of her gunners in their anti-flash suits doubling to the corvette's guns.

Colonel Savage frowned and somewhere close by Peewee said happily, '*Hot shit*! Looks like I'm gonna get me some action at last, Colonel, sir.'

Savage didn't answer. He couldn't.

CHAPTER 12

'*Starboard thirty*!' the skipper of the *Azalea* screamed as he saw the white blur of the torpedoes racing straight towards the corvette. 'Engine room … smoke at the double, *we're under attack!*'

As thick black smoke began to pour from the *Azalea's* stacks, Barthels's E-boat raced towards the corvette yet again, the torpedo men tensed over their deadly steel fish. Great white bow waves flew from her stern. She heeled in a crazy turn, her starboard guard-rails disappearing under the water for an instant. There were two soft thuds, followed by the noise of the torpedoes plopping into the raging sea. Then the E-boat was surging away at top speed, followed by the shells of *Azalea's* 4.5 inch guns.

Now as the E-boat rushed for safety, her *Vierling* flak gun opened up, white tracer shells hissing towards the English ship at a thousand rounds a minute. They riveted a line along the corvette's length. A lookout dropped from the yards like a bird hit on the wing and then the *Azalea* disappeared into her own smoke and *Kapitänleutnant* Barthels knew he had failed to sink her. The Tommy was still afloat. Now there was only one thing left for him to do, while the rest of his flotilla disengaged itself from that damned merchant convoy which had confused them totally; he had to lure the sole escort away from the landing barges. Perhaps the Big Lion's super-ace might be able to sink one of the transports and carry out the job his flotilla had apparently failed to do.

He frowned and then did it. As a piece of spent shell fragment slammed against the side of his helmet and would have sent him reeling if he had not grabbed the wheel in time, he swung the E-boat round once more and bounded forward, right into the hail of fire coming from the Tommy…

'Stand by, engine room!' Otto commanded. Ahead, one of the huge landing craft was wallowing heavily from side to side, as if the helmsman was drunk. Otto lowered his binoculars, satisfied that the escort had gone. The big fat beauty was all his for the taking. He threw a splash of cheap cologne onto his silk muffler to kill the stink of oil and vomit. He rapped out a series of quick orders. The E-boat swung round so that it faced the unsuspecting enemy directly midships.

Otto knew he was going to die young. He had already decided that as a seventeen-year-old cadet. '*Live a good life and make a handsome corpse,*' had been his motto, always. Now, he seized the bottle of cheap *Korn* from the rack and took a stiff drink. He felt the fiery spirit slam against his gullet and burn its way down to his ruined stomach. 'That'll keep the puke down for a while at least,' he said to no one in particular and then concentrated on the task ahead.

His attack tactics would be simple — and dangerous. He would race in at forty knots an hour, using the boat itself as a direction finder for his 'kippers', as he called his torpedoes airily. He would not fire them till he was five hundred metres away. It would be unfortunate if the transport were armed. 'Hard shit,' he grinned to himself, then yelled, the adrenalin pumping through his blood-stream, 'Engine room … give me all you've got… *Full speed ahead!*'

The E-boat lurched forward. The roar of the motors was tremendous. The very air quivered. A huge white wave sprang up on both sides like a pair of swan's wings. The deck tilted speedily, as the bow rose from the water. On the dripping deck, the torpedo mate steadied himself, as the boat trembled beneath him like a live thing. The transport grew bigger and bigger. It seemed to fill the whole horizon. *Would that crazy young bastard at the wheel never give the frigging order to fire the kippers?*

'FIRE!' Otto shrieked. '*ONE… TWO…!*'

The E-boat shuddered violently. For an instant Otto could see the sleek kippers flashing into the boiling sea and then he was hurtling the boat round, already fumbling with trembling fingers for his binoculars, body tensed for the shock-wave of the explosions.

Nothing happened!

Otto stared open-mouthed as the big transport sailed on, lazy white tracer curving its way in graceful arcs towards the little craft. The kippers had failed to explode! With a sinking feeling he told himself the frogs had been up to their old tricks once again. They had sabotaged the warheads. Now what was he going to frigging well do? Almost unconsciously, he reached out for the bottle of *Korn*.

Savage flung up his glasses, as above him on the bridge the machine guns chattered urgently and everywhere his men were flinging themselves to the deck, hands on their helmets. All was chaos and confusion out to sea. Star shells exploded in bursts of bright silver. Tracer zipped back and forth in multicoloured splendour. The roar of high-speed motors mingled with the yammer of guns firing at a tremendous rate. Now he knew this was the real thing. The Krauts were attacking both convoys. Somewhere a flak-cannon started to spray the LST with shells. They raced towards the big slow ship like a glowing white wall, roaring in at a tremendous rate. A sailor screamed and went overboard, all flailing arms. A shell exploded nearby, ripping down the wireless masts in a fury of exploding blue sparks. Shrapnel hissed everywhere, fist-sized and glowing and evil-red. A gun crew disappeared, vanished in an instant, to reappear in the boiling water below.

The superstructure was ripped apart by that tremendous barrage. The wires gave. It started to tumble down. Men screamed, trapped beneath the falling debris. Others sank to their knees, grasping their throats, retching and choking in the acrid fumes. Some simply died where they stood, not a mark on their bodies, their lungs ripped apart by the awesome blast of that horrific barrage.

Peewee staggered into view, illuminated by the lurid flames that were springing up everywhere. His helmet was gone and there was something red trickling down the side of his freckled face. He was laughing like a crazy man and in his hand he clutched that big pistol. 'Thought you'd lost me, Colonel, sir?' he cried, his voice distorted and wild.

Savage stared at him in horror, as out to sea the E-boat wheeled in a tremendous burst of wild white water and careened into the attack once more. 'You're drunk, Peewee!' he rasped, no longer afraid of the little Texan, realizing that he had a fatal weakness too. 'You've been drinking!'

'Sure, Colonel, sir,' Peewee chortled happily, slapping his canteen with his free hand, 'Had me a little snort, I must admit.' He grinned inanely in that unreal glowing scarlet light. 'Why not? Guy's entitled to a li-ttle pleasure, ain't he, Colonel, Sir?' He raised the pistol. 'But I can still shoot, yessir. Still knock the dong off'n a grasshopper at fifty feet!' He cackled crazily, and Savage knew whatever else happened, he had to get away from Peewee. The little man had the crazed look of the killer in his eyes.

'*Skipper!*' the mate cried fervently, as Otto started to turn the sinking E-boat with hands that were already blood-red claws. 'You can't —'

'Leave me alone!' Otto snarled, 'Leave me frigging well alone!' His knees sagged a little more and he felt the life-blood running out him rapidly. The burst he had taken in the chest had finished him off, exactly as he had always imagined it would happen to him. 'Jump over the side if you're scared,' he coughed thickly, and blood trickled down the side of his hairless chin. 'I'm going to get the fucker!' His knees sagged even more and he whispered, 'Please, *Obermaat*, point me in the right direction … and then … you can go!'

'There then, *damn you!*' the petty officer swung the wheel round until the sinking E-boat was facing the blazing LST. A moment later he dived over the side, already practising the little bit of English he knew for his rescuers.

Dimly through half-closed eyes, Otto saw the monstrous black hulk which seemed to fill the whole world. He tore down the throttles, hanging there, dying on his feet. The E-boat responded. She started to gather speed once more and what was left of the deck crew flung themselves overboard, leaving the craft to the dead and dying.

Otto, dying on his feet, hung on desperately. Through the red fog he could see the transport looming up in front of him, growing larger and larger by the instant so that it filled the horizon like a grey mountain. He longed for one last slug of the *Korn*, but he knew he'd never find the controls again if he took his hands off them.

Machine-gun fire ripped the length of the E-boat. That absurd standard came tumbling down. 'My three tits,' he said hopelessly, already drifting off into the black mist of death, as the E-boat reared towards its victim. If only the other two torpedoes exploded with the impact, it would all be worthwhile, he told himself. *Or would it?*

That last burst of desperate fire hit him like a gigantic fist. The impact was so tremendous that he gasped out loud. Bone splintered. His blood splattered the littered deck in bright red gobs. Far, far away he could hear himself screaming. His helpless shattered body slammed onto the heaving plates, urine and faeces streaming down his legs. For one fleeting moment his young face softened into a kind of weary smile. Next moment he died and the E-boat careened into the side of the transport with the force of a monstrous factory hammer.

For what seemed an age, the E-boat just wallowed there purposelessly, her bow crumpled like a banana skin, a mass of torn and twisted smoking metal, dead men sprawled on her shattered deck like broken toys cast away by a careless spoilt child. Up above, the whistles shrilled. Officers shrieked urgent orders. Boat chains rattled furiously, while soldiers stared down at the dead Germans below in numb disbelief. Then it happened. There was a muffled crump. The E-boat disintegrated, not quickly, but as if in slow motion, her stern rearing high into the air, screws spinning uselessly in the glowing darkness.

The LST appeared undamaged, save for the great jagged hole in her side. Savage thought with the rest they were going to make it after all. The E-boat's torpedoes had failed to explode. The unknown German skipper had sacrificed his life for nothing.

Then with startling suddenness, the LST's main magazine exploded. The big ship was racked from stem to stern. Great gleaming metal fissures were running the length of her deck abruptly. The superstructure creaked alarmingly and began to tumble in a mass of angry blue sparks. Smoke belched from her one stack. Tracer ammunition zig-zagged crazily straight into the sky like a Fourth of July fireworks' display and in a flash panic-stricken voices were crying everywhere, 'Abandon ship… *ABANDON SHIP!*'

Five hundred metres away, the awed, silent deck crew of Century One felt the shock, as if someone had just punched them in the guts — *hard*, as that main magazine exploded. Now the stern of the LST was rearing high into the darkness like a great steel tomb. Slowly, inexorably, the bows started to slide beneath the waves, which leapt up greedily to receive her, only to recoil the next instant, hissing and spluttering angrily, as if they could feel the searing heat of her red-hot plates.

Then, in one last wild tumult of water, she was gone, and for the first time the U-boat crew were aware that the sea all around was filled with desperate, screaming men.

Christian shook his head as if trying hard to awake from a deep sleep. 'Stand by with the boat-hooks down there!' he called from the bridge.

'Ay, ay, sir!' von Cheetham, in charge of the rescue party, answered. A little further beyond, Frenssen, towering above his gun crew, all of them armed with rifles and sub-machine guns, yelled, 'Gun crew all present and correct, sir!'

Christian nodded his understanding and yelled to the sailors standing next to him on the conning tower, 'All right, switch on the searchlight, Dietz. Let's start hunting for our damned Bigot and then let's get the holy hell out of here!'

'Sir!'

Dietz clicked on the powerful beam. In a flash its hard, dazzling white light cut the darkness to reveal the indescribable mess in the water around where LST 507 had gone down.

Everywhere there were men bobbing up and down in the water, yelling, waving their hands frantically, trying to keep themselves afloat, desperately trying to shed their heavy equipment before it was too late. Dead men, too, sprawled out on bits of shattered wood, or curled into tight balls, hands clasped tightly to their ears, as if in the moment of death they had tried to cut out the terrible noise. There was even a cat, head sliced off by flying shrapnel, lying in a wicker basket, floating off to nowhere.

'*Swing her round!*' Christian yelled desperately, trying to swallow the bitter bile which threatened to choke him at the terrible sight, ears closed to the cries, the pleas, the broken-hearted weeping. '*Over here,*' they called. '*For God's sake, buddy, over here… Help me, on my mother's name, oh, please, help me… I can't see, you've gotta gimme a hand… I can't see…!*' That piteous litany went on and on.

Now as Dietz swept his searchlight beam slowly from left to right, gaze intent on spotting those silver insignia, which meant so much, the first of the screaming, panic-stricken survivors began to reach the surfaced U-boat. Choking and gasping, black with oil, they reached up from the slick, waving frantically to attract attention. One completely covered with black, teeth a gleaming white, was singing, 'Mami … mami … I'd wait a million years…' and waving crazily, happy in the knowledge that he, at least, had been saved.

But that wasn't to be. Eyes flooded with tears, trembling all over, *Oberleutnant* von Cheetham commanded, 'For God's sake push them away… We can't use them…' He broke off, unable to watch any more, as his sailors placed the long boathooks against the men struggling in the slick and, taking the strain as if they were pushing a punt, forced the terror-stricken survivors away.

Somehow, a few of them managed to creep onto the deck to the port of Century One, advancing out of the darkness like glistening, sleepwalking zombies. Frenssen moaned. '*No … no … no!*' Without even aiming, he pressed the trigger of his machine pistol. It chattered frantically at his side. The Americans went over the side in a mess of flailing arms and legs, their agonized screams killed even before they hit the water. Then the big petty officer slumped against the 88mm cannon and, watched by his horrified crew, began to retch as if he were heart-broken…

Savage heard the sudden burst of machine-gun fire, as all around, the sea swayed and trembled, littered as it was with bits and pieces of flotsam, the banal, pathetic rubbish of a ship's wreck, *and the dead!*

'Stand fast!' he cried to the living, treading water. 'Stand fast the First Battalion!'

But the First Battalion existed no longer and no one was listening to him anymore. What looked like a blackened log bumped into him. He was about to push it away angrily when he recognized it for what it was; the dead colonel of engineers, still wearing his GI glasses, that absurd slide-rule clasped in his dead hands, as a Catholic might clutch his rosary. Gently he disengaged himself from the body. It floated away into the darkness and suddenly he had an eerie feeling it might go on like that, floating around the oceans of the world, for ever.

A man swam by him. In the hard silver light of the searchlight which was scanning the area carefully, parting the oily darkness with cold brilliant fingers, he could see his face, the eyes crazy and blood-shot, foam oozing from mouth and nostrils. He recoiled in horror and trod water again. The man swam on, muttering to himself madly, using great powerful strokes, as if he couldn't reach the place he was going to die quickly enough.

Savage considered. He had seen it all before. His landing barge had been hit and swamped at Anzio. Most of the men around him were going to be dead before dawn. Exposure or their very equipment would kill them before the rescue ships arrived. He'd die, too; he had no illusions about that. Unless…

What had the Englishwoman said that last night (he still couldn't bring himself even now to call her May)? *Only characters in cheap novels are condemned right from the start. Oh, Sam, there is a way out!'*

'*A way out … a way out … a way out…*' the words echoed and re-echoed around and around the depths of his brain. Somewhere someone was singing crazily, '*Rock of ages… rock of ages…*'

'*Of course, I don't need to fucking well die!*' Sam Savage rasped suddenly, new energy surging through his body, voice full of sudden hope. 'Why should I?' He knew they were shooting over the heads of the enlisted men to keep them away from the sub. But they wouldn't at him. They'd see his insignia and recognize him for an officer. The Germans always wanted officers. Because of their own strict caste system, they always thought officers were the only ones in the Army who knew anything of value for Intelligence. He chuckled to himself. Little did they know what he really knew, but of course they'd never get *that* from him!

'Repent before it is too late.' The man who had been singing came into view, one charred hand raised like a Biblical prophet. 'The end is nigh… Repent before it is too late!' He tried to hold on to the colonel. Savage smashed up his hand, palm uppermost, and caught the crazy man just beneath the nose. He went spluttering backwards into the slick, warning cut off abruptly. Next moment Savage struck out for the sub, crying, 'Here I am … here I am… A colonel of infantry, I demand to speak to your skipper…'

'*There*!' Christian called urgently. 'Dietz, for God's sake hold that frigging beam straight!'

Dietz fumbled frantically with the bridge searchlight, and there he was. There was no mistaking that silver star. 'It's one of them, sir,' he gasped, ignoring the horror all around in the black sea below. '*It's a Bigot*!'

Christian didn't hesitate. He cupped his hands around his mouth and yelled above the screams, the pleas, the curses in the water below, '*Oberleutnant* von Cheetham, do you see him? Over there… Grab that one!'

Von Cheetham, shaken as he was by those terrible sights, reacted at once. 'Boat crew,' he commanded, 'get that one… Come on. *Dalli … dalli*, fish that one out!'

The greenbeaks needed no urging. They had seen enough. They wanted to get their Ami and submerge, escape this murderous place of absolute horror. Leaning out dangerously, they extended their long, brass-tipped poles towards the man swimming powerfully through the slick, that silver star gleaming in the harsh white glare of the searchlight. Weakly leaning against the cannon, Frenssen watched, trembling all over, his big fingers clasped together like an old, old granny praying fervently that miracles still might happen.

'*Cocksucker*!' Peewee, sitting on his float, cursed, half-drunk, half-mad, oblivious to the death and destruction all around him, red-rimmed eyes blazing with fury. '*The goddam Yankee cocksucker*!'

He watched as the colonel struck out so confidently for the German sub, and told himself it had always been that way. In the end, the rich always bugged out and left the poor to pick up the frigging pieces.

Back as a kid in Texas, knee-high to a grasshopper, while the sun had beaten down remorselessly and the cotton had seemed endless, he had dreamed of faraway battlefields, where the bugles had shrilled, the banners had streamed and brave men had charged gallantly across the flaming hills of the South. But those dreams, he had soon realized, were not for his sort, the son of a poor goddam share-cropper; they had been for high-falutin' gentlemen in Dallas, who held the purse-strings, high-falutin' city gents from the North, just like the colonel.

For poor 'white trash', share-cropping farmers like his folks, the goddam weeds had been the enemy, the hoe their weapon, their only banner a dream that they might, one day, escape that back-breaking existence. But they never had. Those high-falutin' gents, those money-bags from the North, with their letters-of-credit, mortgages, threats of foreclosure, had seen to that. They had died as they had lived — in poverty, miserable, while the Northern landlords had prospered.

He raised the pistol. It was the only thing that cut the difference between them and him down to size. 'Good ole forty-five!' he crooned crazily and took a bead on the swimming man. '*Cocksucker — die!*' He started to take first pressure.

Oberleutnant von Cheetham realized immediately what the lone American on the float was going to do. He knew it instinctively. '*Obermaat,*' he yelled urgently to Frenssen standing by the cannon, 'that Ami —'

His words ended in a scream of pain as his chest exploded and he was slammed against the conning tower, as if propelled there by a giant fist, dying on his feet.

Savage shook the water from his face. It was that little Texan bastard who had fired. It was Peewee again. He trod water desperately. 'Peewee!' he called.

'Yes, Colonel, *sir*!' He could hear the fake cynical politeness and knew that the Englishwoman was wrong. There was no escape.

On the bridge Christian watched the two of them, faces hollowed out to death masks by the bright white light of the searchlight. What was going on? What was the Bigot (for he was one, Christian knew that) shouting at the other Ami? Was he mistaken, but there seemed a note of pleading in the colonel's voice? Suddenly he gasped with horror. The man on the float, cackling crazily, was raising that big pistol again — *and he was pointing it directly at the man treading water*!

'Dietz!' he yelled desperately, 'Switch the beam. Blind the bastard —'

'*NO!*' Savage screamed.

Too late! Drunk and crazy as he was, Peewee didn't miss. The slug hit the man in the water right between the eyes, just below the helmet with the silver star.

Five minutes later Century One had gone in a wild tumult of white water, leaving the sea empty save for a mass of floating debris and the lone man on the rubber float, sobbing, sobbing, as if his very heart would break...

ENVOI

'Emergency, sir … emergency, sir… *Wake up*!'

Christian groaned and sat up in bed. His head still ached from the party of the previous night in the old part of Brest. There had been lobster and champagne, plenty of it, and girls, too, *willing* French girls; it had almost been like old times. One might have thought that Germany was still the all-conquering victor, master of the whole of Europe from the Channel to the Volga. 'What is it, steward?' he called thickly, feeling his head throb painfully.

'The Allies have come, sir!' the little man called from the other side of the door, the customary mincing tone absent from his voice. They said he did a tremendous imitation of Marlene Dietrich when he was in the mood, all blond wig and sheer black stockings.

'*What*?'

'The Anglo-Americans have landed. It's just come over the wire, sir!'

'Where?' he rasped, suddenly very awake.

'Normandy, sir,' and then he was gone to hammer on the door of the next room.

Christian puffed out his cheeks. 'So the clock is really in the pisspot!' he said to the darkened room. 'Rundstedt was wrong and they've caught him with his knickers down about his ankles.' With a groan, he swung himself out of his bed and walked unsteadily to the blacked-out window. He drew the curtain and peered down at his watch. It was three-thirty. 'Three-thirty, June sixth, 1944,' he said to the silent room, 'A significant date, no doubt!'

The room didn't reply, as if it was nodding a silent assent to his statement.

Christian, still slightly drunk, grinned, as the moonlight flooded in. In books, they said, one always remembered such historic dates. '*June sixth, 1944.*' He savoured the words. Would he? Would he remember this date in years to come? He doubted it. By that time he would be dead, for sure. He gave a wry, crooked grin at the thought and gazed out at the port, and beyond the sea. It was perfectly peaceful. Up the coast men were dying violently, thousands of them. But here all was calm and silent, the full moon bathing the waves a bright beautiful silver.

He thought of all that suffering, all that effort. Trainburster Thomas … *Oberleutnant* von Cheetham … that dying Ami colonel sinking beneath the waves, a bloody hole neatly and surprisingly drilled beneath that vital silver star … the crazy, drunken soldier as his float had disappeared into the night, as if he might wander the oceans for ever like the flying Dutchman… What had it all meant? What was its significance?

'*Nothing!*' the cynical little voice at the back of his mind answered his unspoken question. '*Absolutely, fucking nothing…!*' '*Nussbraun muss mein Madel sein … so wie ich…*' that well-known voice cut into his sad reverie drunkenly.

He craned his neck. It was Frenssen all right. Drunk as usual, a struggling woman, a French whore probably, slung over one shoulder, another hooked under his arm, with behind him a one-legged sailor in striped hospital pyjamas lugging a sack obviously filled with bottles.

Frenssen saw him. He tried to click to attention and nearly fell over with the effort. 'All men — er — women on board, sir!' he cried uproariously. 'Boat is ready for patrol!' He let go of the one whore and slapped the fat silken bottom of the one slung over his shoulder happily. 'And what a patrol this is going to be!'

Behind him the one-legged refugee from the naval hospital automatically took yet another bottle from his sack, broke off the neck on his wooden leg and offered it politely to Frenssen. 'More fire-water, *Herr Obermaat*,' he quavered.

Frenssen accepted it, took a great swig and flung it away, roaring, '*Gnats' piss*! Ain't you got anything stronger? And quick or I'll stick yer wooden leg up yer ass and make yer eyes pop out!'

Christian didn't give him a chance to carry out that terrible threat. Down in the port the air-raid sirens were already sounding their dread warning. He could hear the running feet, too, and the excited calls. 'Frenssen, drop that woman!' he commanded sharply. 'You, sailor,' he called to the one-legged one in hospital pyjamas. 'Get back to the *Lazarett*!'

'Yes, sir, thank you, sir.' The one-legged sailor dropped the sack of bottles, as if they were red-hot. They splintered into a mass of wet, broken glass and then he was hopping away happily into the night.

'All that sauce!' Frenssen moaned, lowering the drunk whore, while the other sagged against his massive frame, as someone might against a mighty oak.

'Fuck the sauce!' Christian said crudely. 'Get rid of the women. Round up the crew!'

'Women … crew…?' Frenssen's eyes clicked back and forth like a spectator at a tennis match.

'Yes, you heard me, plush-ears! We're getting out of here while we've still got a chance, before…' A group of officers with the red stripe of the Greater German General Staff down the side of their elegant breeches were running heavily through the moonlight to a waiting car, its nervous driver gunning its engine furiously as if the new invaders were just behind him. Christian told himself that the first of the rats were leaving the sinking ship.

'But where are we going to go, sir?' Frenssen asked plaintively, idly fondling the whore's plump, silken bottom like a housewife reluctantly letting go of some choice piece of fruit she couldn't afford.

'Into the open sea ... anywhere, away from here ... Now get rid of those whores... *Move it!*'

'*Adieu mesdames,*' Frenssen boomed in his atrocious French. 'The course of true love never did run straight.' Gallantly he bent and kissed each of them on the hand, then he was running, lurching alarmingly, into the glowing darkness to muster the crew, leaving the two whores staring at his back in absolute bewilderment.

For a moment more, Christian remained at the window, listening to the drumroll of the flak across the bay, watching the scarlet flame stab the darkness, brain racing electrically. They had landed at last and they wouldn't be thrown back into the sea, he knew that. Germany had lost the war. There was no hope now, and in a way the thought was comforting. He knew exactly where he stood, how the course of the rest of his young life would run, before it happened to him, too. Almost happily, *Kapitänleutnant* Christian Jungblut began to fling himself into his uniform, while the guns rolled and thundered. The sea was waiting for him again and at sea there was always just a chance...

A NOTE TO THE READER

Dear Reader,

If you have enjoyed this novel enough to leave a review on **Amazon** and **Goodreads**, then we would be truly grateful.

Sapere Books

Sapere Books is an exciting new publisher of brilliant fiction and popular history.

To find out more about our latest releases and our monthly bargain books visit our website:
saperebooks.com